hashbROwn Winters

and the

Mashimoto Madness

To Riley,
Keep reading!

hashbrown winters

and the

Mashimoto Madness

Frank L. Cole

Bonneville Books
Springville, Utah

The views expressed within this work are the sole responsibility of the author and do not necessarily reflect the position of Cedar Fort, Inc., or any other entity.

This is a work of fiction. The characters, names, incidents, places, and dialogue are products of the author's imagination, and are not to be construed as real.

ISBN 13: 978-1-59955-378-8

Published by Bonneville Books, an imprint of Cedar Fort, Inc., 2373 W. 700 S., Springville, UT 84663
Distributed by Cedar Fort, Inc., www.cedarfort.com

LIBRARY OF CONGRESS CATALOGING-IN-PUBLICATION DATA

Cole, Frank, 1977-
  Hashbrown Winters and the Mashimoto madness / written by Frank L. Cole ; illustrated by Adam Record.
    p. cm.
  Summary: Hashbrown Winters and his friends foil an evil plot by a fellow student to take over Pordunce Elementary School.
  ISBN 978-1-59955-378-8
  [1. Schools--Fiction. 2. Humorous stories.] I. Record, Adam, ill. II. Title.

  PZ7.C673435Has 2010
  [Fic]--dc22

       2009042792

Illustrations by Adam Record
Cover design by Jen Boss
Cover design © 2010 by Lyle Mortimer
Edited and typeset by Heidi Doxey

Printed in the United States of America
10 9 8 7 6 5 4 3 2 1

Printed on acid-free paper

To my mother, for helping me overcome
my fear of flyswatters.

Praise for *The Adventures of Hashbrown Winters*

Hashbrown, Snow Cone, Four Hips, Whiz, and the rest of his friends will have you laughing out loud. Frank L. Cole has created a wonderfully funny story with enough twists and turns to keep children and adults glued to their seats.

    J. Scott Savage,
    author of the Farworld series

An excellent book. You'll be laughing a lot as you sit on the edge of your seat. Highly recommended.

    James Dashner,
    author of The 13th Reality series

★ ★ ★

Praise for *Hashbrown Winters and the Mashimoto Madness*

Hashbrown Winters and the Mashimoto Madness is one enjoyable adventure. So good in fact I almost overlooked what a master Frank is with using capital letters at the start of each sentence. You're going to love this book.

    Obert Skye,
    author of the Leven Thumps series

Filled with crazy, hare-brained, witty humor that just sort of reaches from out of nowhere and smacks you right in the face when you're least expecting it! It will have you smiling, wincing, laughing, and downright snorting out loud before you are finished.

    Phillip J. Chipping,
    CEO, www.knowonder.com

Acknowledgments

First and foremost, I have to thank my wife, Heidi, for encouraging me to take dangerous leaps, despite how clumsy I am. Thanks to my folks, the Coles and the Hickoks, for not acting so surprised that I actually wrote something worth reading.

To my friends at Deseret Book, especially those at the Fort (you know who you are), thanks for selling Hashbrown with reckless abandon. Thank you to Lyle, Jennifer, Sheralyn, Liz, and Heidi for taking yet another chance on that goofy kid from Pordunce. And a big thanks to Adam Record, my illustrator, whose artistic vision helped give life to Hashbrown.

I'm grateful for my brother, Michael, the genius storyteller, who went without sleep to listen to my late-night readings, and for my sister, Jennifer, who, despite being on the verge of tackling the publishing world, took time to point me in the right direction.

Thanks to my neighbors in Valley Ridge who made sure I wasn't all by myself for my very first book signing.
I'll never forget you!

Acknowledgments

And I have to give a big thanks to the new friends I've made at all the elementary schools I've visited. The teachers, librarians, and principals are doing amazing things, and the kids (my pals for life) really know how to use their imaginations.

Last but not least, thanks to all the readers who chose to read *Hashbrown*. Your giggles have made another tale possible. I hope I get the chance to keep you laughing!

Contents

Chapter 1
A Sinister Plan

Professor Porch's bald head gleamed like a polished lollipop as he tugged on the corners of his white laboratory jacket. He had an important appointment, and he couldn't be late. After checking his watch and adjusting his sunglasses on the bridge of his nose, he knocked on the office door.

"It's open!" a voice shouted from the other side. Professor Porch's hands nearly fumbled his clipboard as he took a deep breath and walked into the office.

A massive desk sat across the room, covered with top secret documents, baseball cards, and candy wrappers. A leather chair faced the far wall where a plasma television screen played a cartoon movie.

"Ah, Professor Porch, you're early," a young voice said from behind the leather chair. "Tell me you have good news. Is everything going as planned with the experiment?"

"Yes, sir," Professor Porch said. He held up a flask filled with bright blue liquid. "We tried out the secret potion on our test subjects, and the results were amazing."

"Really? Amazing?" The chair swiveled, allowing Porch a clear view of the boy sitting there; his feet didn't quite reach the floor. He grabbed the flask out of the professor's hand and held it up to the light. "What exactly will they do?"

"There's no limit to what we can have them do," Porch said. "They will attack anyone and anything with just a simple command. Their minds are completely under our control, and they have no power to resist once they've taken the potion. They're very quick to respond. Oh, and they also fetch newspapers." Professor Porch jotted some notes on his clipboard and exhaled with deep satisfaction.

"Excellent!" the boy said. "Soon, we will be ready to take—wait a minute." He pressed the mute button on his remote control, and the cartoon fell silent. "Did you just say 'fetch newspapers'?"

"Uh . . . er . . . yes, sir." Porch fidgeted with his papers, crinkling up the top page. "What I meant to say—"

"Porch!" the boy barked. "Who are you using as your test subjects?"

Professor Porch flipped a page on his clipboard. "Dogs, sir. We're using dogs."

"You're using *dogs* for our experiment?"

"Uh, yes. But I promise you we should see the same results with human subjects."

"Show me," the boy demanded. He pointed his stubby finger at the television screen.

Professor Porch walked over to the entertainment center and pressed a button, switching the screen from the movie to a view of a laboratory testing room. The boy's eyes lit up with interest as he watched a row of three grey-haired dogs standing zombielike in the room. Lying around the dogs were numerous chew toys, water bowls, and dog biscuits. The three dogs stood still, ignoring the items and staring only at the window.

"They're schnauzers, sir," Professor Porch whispered. "Fine dogs, indeed. They are purebreds and are paper trained. The little one's named Pablo." For some odd reason, that dog was wearing a bright red baseball cap.

There was a long silence as the boy stared at each of the dogs. "So these dogs will do whatever is asked of them?"

Professor Porch nodded and plucked a tiny radio from his coat pocket. "Proceed with the demonstration," he said into the microphone.

On the television screen, a man dressed in a suit of armor wobbled into the room. He tried to stand still, but his knees were shaking.

"Not again," the man whimpered. "I don't get paid enough to do this!"

The dogs stood frozen, still staring at the window. Professor Porch pressed the radio against his lips and spoke. "Mortimer, Suzie, Pablo—attack!"

All three dogs sprang to life, barking and growling. The man in the suit of armor yelped as the dogs circled around him. He tried kicking them away, but the armor was too heavy, and the dogs stood their ground. One by one, they pounced, sending the man crashing to the floor. Suzie and Mortimer stood guard, snarling in the man's face while Pablo carefully picked the wallet out of the man's pocket. As quickly as it had started, the show was over. All three dogs formed a line in the middle of the room.

The boy clapped his hands. "Clever, aren't they?" He smacked the armrest of his chair. "But why a suit of armor?"

"We tried kilts at first, thinking the dogs would feel more at home, but that got somewhat messy. Pablo tends to get a little feisty."

"I see." The boy scratched his chin. "You said they are completely under our control. How much control do we have?"

Porch pressed the microphone of his radio up to his mouth. "Pablo." His voice echoed through the room on the television screen. "Piddle." Pablo immediately charged right for the man, sniffed the man's metal helmet, and raised his leg, ready to strike. The man squealed, preparing for the worst. Just as Pablo was about to carry out the order, Professor Porch spoke into the intercom. "Pablo, I command you to stop!"

Pablo stopped, his furry paw hovering in the air.

"Get back in line with the others."

Pablo obeyed.

"Well done!" the boy cheered. "Now, how sure are you that the potion will have the same effects on humans?"

Professor Porch looked down at his clipboard once again. "Seventy-five percent sure, with only a few known side-effects so far."

"Such as?"

"Well . . . there's about a 15 percent chance the human subjects will disobey direct orders and start to play dress up. That's the reason Pablo is wearing a hat. He couldn't help himself, sir."

"Hmmm, that's good enough for me. Now turn my cartoon back on, please," the boy said.

"Sir, may I ask a question?"

The boy hesitated for a moment, then nodded.

"How do you plan to find humans to use this potion on?"

"I'm glad you asked, Porch, because I have a new assignment for you." The boy's face pulled into a wicked grin. Porch started to scribble on his notepad but was waved off. "No, I don't want you writing this down. It's secret."

"What do you have in mind?" Porch asked.

"From what I hear, you're good at blending in, wearing disguises. Is this true?"

Porch glanced around to make sure they were both still alone. "Well, I suppose I'm fairly good."

"Excellent. Now, for my plan to work, no one can know I'm involved. You have to be extra careful. I don't want anyone figuring out what's going on until it's too late." The boy popped his knuckles in both of his hands. "I'm going to need you to find a way to spread the potion to everyone at Pordunce Elementary—the principal, teachers, lunch ladies, janitors, and especially the students. Don't miss a single one. Spread it throughout the town if you have to. Go to where they hangout: the grocery store, the shopping malls. I want the whole school."

"The school?" Professor Porch asked. "What's so important about Pordunce Elementary?"

The boy's eyes fell across the room to where a banquet table held plates of cookies, brownies, and punch. There were several chairs seated around the table, but all were empty. Professor Porch followed his gaze.

"No one came to your little get-together, did they?" he asked.

"No," the boy answered quietly. "They're always too busy with try-outs and initiations to share a few snacks with me." He pouted, but then shook his head and slapped his hand over his forehead. "I don't want to talk about that! Just do as you're told." The boy turned the volume up on the television. "Soon, if all goes as planned, everyone at Pordunce Elementary will be under my command. Then, I'll take on the world!"

Chapter 2
Candy Cannons and Petting Zoos

The hallways at Pordunce Elementary were filled with students of various shapes and sizes hurrying toward classrooms as the first period bell clanged overhead. Everyone was excited for the weekend. I caught a glimpse of Misty Piccolo tiptoeing by, and for a brief moment our eyes met. Her eye lashes fluttered, and I felt woozy. She was the girl of my dreams and had actually been my girlfriend for about a week. Was she really smiling? Maybe she was finally going to forgive me for ruining our science project which earned us a solid C-.

Misty stuck out her tongue in disgust. I must have looked like a moron, smiling as she flipped her hair in my face and pranced away. Why was she being so immature? It was going to break my heart to have to pelt her with a spit wad. I quickly rummaged through my backpack for some ammunition, but groaned as she vanished from view into her classroom. I returned my attention to my locker. There would be other opportunities. Oh, yes. The day was still young.

At the moment, I was annoyed by all the distractions, especially since I had to be cautious while opening my locker. For my birthday, my parents bought me the rarest action figure ever. Brody the Ape-Slayer—complete with three authentic ninja throwing stars—was the coolest gift I had ever opened. Everybody wanted to hold it. I'd even had to install a security system for my locker just to protect it.

My fingers trembled as I reworked the combination for the fourth time, taking extra precaution not to trigger the—

"Can I please see it, Hashbrown?"

I screeched and dropped to my knees just as a miniature blow dart shot out from the opening in my locker with lightning speed, sticking into Camo Phillips' shoulder. He collapsed unconscious to the floor. I hadn't even seen him standing there, but that was Camo's specialty. He could be standing in front of a white movie screen, holding a pink umbrella and no one would see him.

Sighing in frustration, I dragged Camo's limp body over to the side and stacked him next to the others. This was getting ridiculous. Eventually, I would have to explain to someone why there was a growing pile of students sleeping next to my locker.

I peered in the locker at my treasure. There he was, The Ape-Slayer, still in his original packaging, resting beneath a crystal dome. I smiled at the package as though it were a newborn baby. Oh, how I wanted to hold it, but for now that was impossible. For one thing, there were too many students around, and for another, I had forgotten how to switch off the parameter alarm. The last thing I needed was a visit to the school nurse because of tear gas exposure.

You're probably wondering, what kind of wacko goes to such extremes to protect a toy? Well, I'm Hashbrown Winters; my name alone explains that I live on the edge. It's a dangerous world, and you can't be too careful. Especially at Pordunce, where there's never an ordinary day. Well, I guess if you consider launching a catapult filled with dill dip at your principal while he's riding bareback on an emu an ordinary day, then maybe you'd understand. Pordunce is filled with unusual kids—some of them dangerous, some of them downright frightening. Luckily, you can usually tell by their names what kind of characters they are. Take my name for example: Hashbrown. I imagine you think of someone cool and athletic. Maybe you see a born leader who's not afraid of an adventure, and of course, someone who can stomach twenty pounds of hash browns in one sitting. Yeah, that's me.

The late bell for first period chimed, and I shuddered. I was going to fail my grammar test because I hadn't studied. Just then Moses Merryweather, a very odd fourth-grader, walked past, his purple robes swishing at his feet.

"Oh great," I muttered as Moses halted and stared at me solemnly.

Holding out his hand just above my eyebrows, he moaned. "You shall score a B+ on your exam, my son." One of his white eyebrows cocked. "Next time, you won't be so lucky." With that, Moses continued down the hallway, pausing now and then to prophesy to his classmates. I rolled my eyes. Moses was always doing that. He got his nickname right after he set his neighbor's bushes on fire and then found a twenty dollar bill wadded up in the garbage. He called it fate, a miracle, maybe even a calling. Since then, he's always making unwanted prophecies, but most of the time he's wrong.

★ ★ ★

Sure enough, one hour later, I walked out with a D and an angry note for my parents from Mr. Coppercork. How was I supposed to know that the apple I gave him was infested with earwigs? It was an innocent mistake.

Snow Cone Jones joined me at the drinking fountains. "You got a D?" he asked, stifling his laughter and choking on a swig of water. "Even Measles got a B, and he spilled anti-itch cream on his paper." Measles Mumphrey, another one of my closest friends, had an itching problem. Getting measles four times definitely created a miserable rash.

I fidgeted with my backpack zipper. "Lay off, Snow, I had a bad morning." Snow Cone was my best friend and my right hand man in my tree house club. We did everything together and stuck by each other's side through thick and thin.

Snow Cone rummaged in his backpack for a moment. "Check this out." He handed me an envelope with Top Secret stamped in red ink across the front.

"What's this?" I opened the clasp and checked over my shoulder for any suspicious characters. The coast was clear for the most part. Pigeon Criggle was starting to flutter in my direction, but someone opened the main entry doors and a burst of wind shot through the hall, sending him off course. He ended up wedged between the vending machines.

Inside the envelope, I discovered a set of blueprints. I couldn't read the words because they were written in Japanese, but I knew exactly what it was. These were the blueprints for a new tree house. Not my tree house, mind you. No, these were the plans for Hi Mashimoto's new tree house, and it was certain to be a masterpiece.

"How did you get these?" I asked. "And is that what I think it is?" I pointed to an image on the print.

"One of our new recruits swiped it yesterday from Mashimoto's motorbike. He made a copy and returned it before anyone was the wiser. And yes, that's an elevator."

I blinked for several moments. "Big deal," I said, but inside I could feel my blood morphing into spicy barbecue sauce.

Hi Mashimoto had been just your typical fifth grader until a few months ago when he inherited millions of dollars from some rich uncle that had died in Tokyo. Since then, Hi had started showing up to school with fancy new equipment. First, there was the motorbike with a side car. Then, Mashimoto showed up sporting a new laser-powered watch. And now the tree house.

Don't get me wrong, it doesn't bother me when one of my classmates gets a new toy. I'm usually the one that's the first in line to celebrate along with them. It's just that Mashimoto was starting a new club, and he was trying to get my friends to join. Before he came into all his money, no one would've cared about him building a new tree house. Now, everyone was buzzing. It was going to be the most awesome tree house ever constructed. I had gone through too much, building my club into the most talked about establishment in school history, to allow some wannabe to come in and destroy everything. Hi Mashimoto was definitely a threat.

I sighed and handed the blueprints back to Snow Cone. "So he gets a new tree house. Good for him. I don't care."

"You should care," Snow Cone said. "It's going to be the coolest tree house ever."

"Thanks, Snow, you're a real pal."

"All I'm saying is that the competition is becoming steep. Mashimoto's sure to have enough toys to make every first through sixth grader want to hang out with him. This could seriously change our summer plans."

"Can we talk about something else?" I bent over to fix the strap on my Velcro sneakers.

"Like what?"

I tensed as Hambone Oxcart, the scariest student in the school, rumbled past, an aroma of cedar shavings and aftershave tailing on the wind. Snow Cone fell silent as we watched the giant pause at the drinking fountain. After several loud slurps, Hambone trudged on, not looking anyone in the eye, which wasn't saying much, since Hambone towered a foot above the teachers.

"He's not doing well, is he?" Snow Cone whispered.

I shook my head. Two weeks ago Hambone and Luinda "The Manatee" Sharpie, broke up. It was a bad omen. I had a showdown with Hambone on the playground once because I accidentally squashed his pet cockroach. If it hadn't been for Luinda, I would've been playing the harp at the Pearly Gates right now. Well, maybe not the harp, I'm not very good with music. More like a kazoo.

When Hambone and Luinda were together, it was safe to walk the halls at Pordunce. You kept your lunch money and avoided having your arms ripped off. I just hoped Hambone wouldn't return to his old ways of wreaking havoc. I shivered, but only because Whiz Peterson joined us at my locker. Whiz had a way of making one shiver.

"What's going on guys?" Whiz asked, following our gaze down the hall to where Hambone was turning the corner.

I looked down at Whiz's yellow galoshes pulled over the ends of his pant legs. Whiz has a bladder issue; we'll leave it at that for now.

"Snow was about to read off our agenda for tonight," I said, looking at my best friend.

Pulling a clipboard from his backpack, Snow Cone licked his thumb and rifled through a notepad. "We have our usual club meeting after dinner, and the new recruits are scheduled for their initiation. Hummus Laredo is giving a seminar on why we should always eat soybeans for breakfast, and Butter Bibowski and Yeti Mckean are performing a skit."

My tree house was getting crowded. After my battle with Hambone, more and more kids wanted to join. We had our regulars: Me, Snow Cone, Whiz, Measles, Bubblegum, and Four Hips. Those guys had been with me since the dawn of time. To add to that, Pigeon Criggle, a miniature first grader with the power of flight on a windy day had joined recently. So had Paul "The Shiek" Rumspill until Principal Herringtoe discovered a typo on his birth certificate. Now The Shiek is a junior in high school.

"Busy night," Whiz said, checking his watch. "Hey, do you think we can schedule an hour or so for a break at around . . . seven?"

"What for?" I asked.

"Mashimoto is having a party tonight to celebrate the construction of his new tree house, and he's rented a humongous bounce house. There's going to be a petting zoo with real live chimpanzees, and waffle cone sundaes, and some guy that can eat his own foot." Whiz rubbed his hands together.

"If you want to go to Mashimoto's little party, that's up to you, and while you're at it, why don't you join his club as well?" I strapped my backpack to my shoulders and started down the hallway.

"Why, is he recruiting?" Whiz had an almost hopeful tone in his voice.

"Not cool, Whiz, definitely not cool," Snow Cone said. "Besides, I don't think your mother would approve of you playing in a bounce house. Remember what happened last time?"

Whiz frowned. "That was last year, and I'll wear my rubber pants this time. What's wrong with you, Hashbrown?" Whiz jogged up beside me.

"Nothing," I lied.

★ ★ ★

Later that evening, I sat in a recliner in my tree house with a can of soda in my hand, listening to Four Hips chomp down a family-sized carton of croutons. He was on a diet. I looked around and frowned. My tree house was in desperate need of repairs. The rope ladder was beginning to fray, some of the planks in the floor were busted, and Measles' herb garden was running low on oregano. We didn't even have wireless Internet for crying out loud.

" . . . and that's why I suggest if it's not tofu, it's just goo," Hummus concluded. Everyone in the room applauded. From outside came the growing roar of Mashimoto's festival. Whiz was at the window, adjusting his binoculars.

"Oh, man. Now they're shooting off candy cannons!" he shouted.

"Get away from the window," Snow Cone ordered.

Whiz sulked as he sat back down in his kiddy pool.

I crunched my soda can and tossed it out the window to the dumpster down below. "Next order of business," I said.

Snow Cone nodded. "Right. Will the new recruits please stand?" The room fell silent as Hummus Laredo, Butter Bibowski, and Yeti Mckean rose from their chairs.

"What are you doing?" I asked. My mind swirled as more explosions ignited from Mashimoto's backyard. It was quite the party, and it sounded like the entire town had shown up.

"Uh . . . hello?" Snow said, waving his hand in front of my face. My thoughts were elsewhere. "It's time for their initiation."

Why was Mashimoto so lucky? Would I really be jealous once his tree house was finished? So many questions, and I needed answers. I thought I'd make it through the night without giving into the urge to go to Mashimoto's party, but I was wrong. I needed to see for myself what all the fuss was about.

"No!" I shouted, catching everyone off guard. "I'm not in the mood for initiation right now." Slipping on my tennis shoes, I checked my watch. It was almost 8 PM.

"But we practiced our skit all week long!" Butter moaned, throwing his hands up in frustration. "Do you know how hard it is to remember your lines in Polish?" Butter and

Yeti exchanged angry looks. Hummus Laredo was almost in tears. I hadn't seen him this sad since the time he hugged a tree for two straight days only to find out it was really a telephone pole covered in fire ants.

"Don't worry, guys. You're still in the club. There's no need for initiating you tonight." I stared out the window as the sky lit up with fireworks.

"What do you mean?" Snow Cone said. "It's a tradition."

Whiz's head poked up from over the edge of his kiddy pool. "No initiation?" he asked. "We didn't get a chance to spray them with dish soap!" Four Hips and Bulkins groaned their displeasure. Spraying the new recruits was one of their favorite things to do.

Pigeon actually looked relieved. He was the most recent one to be initiated into the club, and some of us had gotten a little carried away. Turns out feathers and dish soap don't mix well.

"Relax, guys," I said, holding my hands out to try and calm the growing uproar. "I'm just in the mood to do something else right now."

"Like what?" Bubblegum asked, bursting a bubble that splattered across his forehead.

"Who's up for a field trip?" I scanned the rows of agitated faces.

"But we haven't got our fake IDs yet," Snow Cone said.

"I'm not talking about the bowling alley, Snow."

"Then what?"

I nodded out the window toward the mushroom cloud of smoke bombs erupting two blocks down, and Whiz started squealing.

"Ah, Hashbrown, you're the best!" Whiz cheered as he accidentally filled up his kiddy pool.

★ ★ ★

MASHIMOTO'S GRAND GALA

★ ★ ★

Chapter 3
Nothing but a Mini-Fridge

I was more than embarrassed walking down to Mashimoto's house. Maybe I was trying to be the bigger person and congratulate Hi. Maybe I just wanted to see what all the fuss was about his party. Whatever the reason, something told me I was about to make one of the biggest mistakes of my life.

Three doors down from my house, and directly next door to Mashimoto's home, was an abandoned shack with faded shutters and an old front door that stood slightly open, giving all who passed a brief glimpse into its eerie darkness. That house had been abandoned for years, and I knew perfectly well it was haunted. I had heard the legends, and I had seen some pretty strange things going on behind those windows. As the last one of my crew walked past the house, an awful moan belched from the windows. The ghosts were having a bad night, and I'd bet my entire marble collection it was because of the ruckus Mashimoto's party was making.

"Tickets please," ordered an old man wearing a tuxedo as we approached the gate to Mashimoto's house. Four Hips looked up at the man blankly and then handed him a chicken salad sandwich wrapper, making sure to snatch a stray piece of lettuce with his fingers. The man grumbled and tossed the trash into the garbage. "Move along, then."

"Tickets?" I asked. "What do you mean tickets?"

"No one gets into Master Mashimoto's Grand Gala without a ticket." The man folded his arms across his chest and glared at me.

I laughed. "See, we can't even go in because we don't have tickets. I guess we're not good enough to be friends with Hi." I turned to leave and gasped as all of my friends produced shiny purple tickets from their trousers. "Wh-what?" I shouted. Whiz handed in his ticket to the man and bounded toward the backyard. I looked desperately at the others. Four Hips, Measles, and Bubblegum stared at their shoes.

"Where did you get those?" I asked.

"Er . . . at Mashimoto's pep rally after lunch," Measles said, scratching a massive boil under his chin. "Didn't you go?"

"Did you see me there?" I snapped.

"Well, not exactly, but Fibber Mckenzie told everyone you were wearing an invisibility cloak."

My mouth dropped open. "When were you going to tell me you had these?" Everyone shrugged their shoulders. "Well, I guess I know whose side you're on. Come on, Snow Cone, let's go get a slurpy." I patted Snow Cone on his shoulder, and he screamed like he was having his ankles amputated.

"I'm sorry, Hashbrown!" In his hand a purple ticket fluttered like a cobra's tongue. "I thought Fibber was probably lying about the invisibility cloak. I should have followed my gut, but Mashimoto promised everyone a free funnel cake if we came before midnight."

I buried my face in my hands. "Not you too, Snow!" Why was this happening to me?

"It doesn't mean anything," Snow said, tugging on my arm. "It was just a stupid mistake."

I felt dizzy, but I knew fainting on the sidewalk in front of everyone was not an option.

"No loitering," the man in the tuxedo growled. "Either turn in your tickets or move out of my way."

"You're right, Snow, it doesn't mean anything. I forgive you," I said. "We all make mistakes. Everyone, let's just go back to my . . ." my voice trailed off as I realized Snow Cone and I were the only two still standing on the opposite side of the gate. All of my other friends were bouncing around the corner in a conga line lead by a fat clown wearing a cape with Mashimoto's face plastered on the back.

"You guys!" I shouted at the top of my lungs. I lunged toward the entrance but fell back when the guard held out his arm to prevent me.

"No one goes in without a ticket." His body, like a gigantic, bloated penguin, completely blocked the way. I wasn't getting in, but now I wanted to more than ever. My shoulders sagged as the end of the conga line vanished from view. The sound of a humming motor rose above the orchestra music, and I looked up as a scooter sputtered to a halt right in front of the gate. Hi Mashimoto dismounted and removed his helmet. He was wearing a golden jumpsuit and pink slippers. Strapped across his back, securely nestled in a knapsack, was what looked like a koala chomping on a eucalyptus leaf.

"What's going on, Sminty?" Mashimoto asked, giving me a withering look.

"Nothing, sir," Sminty said.

"Hello, Snow Cone. How's my good friend been?" Mashimoto beamed from ear to ear.

"Uh . . . um . . . swell," Snow Cone said.

"I trust you're having a grand time at my Grand Gala?" He giggled. "Catchy name huh? Oh, I'm so clever."

"Actually, we were just leaving." I grabbed Snow Cone's arm and started to move away from the gate.

"Leaving? Really? But we've only just started." Mashimoto held out his hands. "There's still the glorious gift exchange. I'm sure Snow Cone would like his present."

I shot a quick glance at Snow Cone, and my heart sunk as I saw his eyes light up at the mention of presents.

He quickly shook away the excitement. "Nah, I don't want any presents," he said. "It's probably just a bunch of cheap, broken toys you could find in a Kid's Meal box." He gave me a reassuring nod.

"On the contrary, I made sure to have the most amazing gifts. Where do you think I got Hampton here?" Mashimoto gestured toward the koala.

"Look, we're leaving. We've got better things to do." I tried to sidestep around Hi.

"Ah, Hashbrown, I heard about the little mix-up with you not having a ticket. That's why I rushed over here to fix it."

My eyes narrowed. "How did you hear about that? We've been here for less than five minutes."

"Gabriel Yucatan told me, of course," Hi said matter-of-factly.

"The Oracle?" Snow Cone gasped. "The Oracle's here?"

Mashimoto waved his hand. "Yes, of course. He wouldn't miss it for the world."

"Oh yeah, where's he now?" I peered over Mashimoto's shoulder, searching for the Oracle.

"He's not here in the way you're thinking. I haven't had any lockers installed yet, but we do have air-conditioning vents."

Gabriel Yucatan, otherwise known as the Oracle, had been stuck in his locker for over seven years. No one I knew had ever seen him face to face. But from what I'd heard, he had glowing red eyes and was paler than a vampire. He had a talent of knowing everything that went on at school. I shuddered as I thought of him lurking in the air-conditioning ducts.

"Sminty, let my two friends in," Mashimoto said.

"But, sir, the saucy one doesn't have a ticket." Sminty jabbed a finger in my direction.

I've been called many things in my life, but I'm pretty certain *saucy* hasn't been one of them. In other circumstances, I might've liked it.

"Don't you know?" Mashimoto bowed reverently in my direction. "Hashbrown's my guest of honor."

Guest of honor? Was that helmet on too tight? We had never been good friends, but we had always treated each other with respect. That was until Mashimoto became an overnight millionaire. From that moment on, whatever respect he had for me was gone. I couldn't walk past his locker without feeling his angry eyes watching me, and I had no idea what I had done to deserve it.

"I'm your guest of honor?" I glanced at Snow Cone who suddenly looked very excited that there was a chance he would make it to the gift exchange.

"Come in and enjoy the party," Mashimoto said. "I want to show you something very special."

At first glance, Mashimoto's house looked no different than the rest of the neighborhood. But it turned out Mashimoto's home expanded beneath the ground for the length of the entire street. It's amazing what a little moolah will buy these days. (That's "money" for those that don't speak German.) For the party, there was a bounce house that could give jackrabbits indigestion, plus a Ferris wheel, a bumper car rink, and a waterslide.

I caught a glimpse of Four Hips guarding the candy cannon with his backside plugging up the hole. He was gobbling up a bucket filled with pudding. Whiz was on the waterslide having a fabulous time because no one dared follow him into the water. I couldn't see the others, but I was sure they were all having the best night of their lives. And to think, I didn't even have a ticket. Oh, how I hated Hi Mashimoto. He was going to ruin everything.

"And over here, you'll see where I intend to assemble my fortress," Mashimoto said, concluding his tour and gesturing toward an area where construction had begun on his tree house. Yellow caution tape hedged up the way, and glowing spot lights shone down from guard towers. It was going to be gigantic. "There will be a marble balcony with a fireman's pole, and if all goes as planned, a landing strip for my jet pack."

Snow Cone choked on his cotton candy. "A jet pack? You have a jet pack?" He looked at me, his eyes wide in amazement.

I looked away. Having a jet pack was kind of a dream of ours. What better way was there to travel?

"Not yet, I'm still in negotiations with the government, but it will be settled soon." Hi watched me for a second and then grinned. "So, Hashbrown, I hear you have a really cool tree house yourself. I've never actually seen it."

I knew by his tone, he was making fun of me. "Yeah, it's a good hideout. Pretty basic." I wanted to get off the subject.

"Tell me, what kind of gadgets do you have?" Mashimoto asked.

"Ah . . . um . . . we have a mini fridge." I looked at Snow Cone for support, but he was too busy gawking at a shaved ice vendor.

"A mini fridge?" Mashimoto chuckled.

"Yeah, you know, it's like a tiny refrigerator you can put sodas and other—"

"I know what it is." Mashimoto rolled his eyes. "*My* tree house will have a stainless-steel refrigerator and a cola dispenser."

I started to sweat, and I could feel something bubbling up inside of me like a casserole. Maybe it was Mom's baked beans, but I knew better. "Really? Well, my tree house has a satellite dish, and we get two hundred and fifty different channels." That was a complete lie. I did have a satellite dish, but it didn't work, and we mostly used it as a massive shield during our water balloon wars every summer.

Mashimoto chortled even louder. "My tree house will have digital cable and a 50-inch plasma television."

I scratched my nose and concentrated on all of the gadgets I currently had in my tree house. There weren't many. "I have a recliner that plays music through the head rest," I said, immediately wishing I hadn't.

"My tree house will have a waterbed with real fish swimming in it."

I almost nodded in approval. That would be awesome, but I didn't dare let Hi see how impressed I was. "Yeah, so, mine has a . . ." I had run out of things to say. Wasn't there anything else? The filing cabinet? No, that was worthless. The trap door that Four Hips had made when we foolishly played hopscotch for a Monday evening activity? No!

Mashimoto seized the opportunity. "Mine will have a telescope that can see Mercury and a radio that can talk to astronauts. Mine will have a pool table and an indoor basketball court. Mine will have a treasure chest filled with real Aztec gold!"

Now he had gone too far. Aztec gold? Come on. He was

bluffing. At least I hoped he was bluffing. I had had enough of the party. It was time to go home, but I just couldn't leave without having the final word. Everything Mashimoto had mentioned was exactly what I had dreamed up for my own tree house. Well, maybe not the pool table. And I had never thought of getting my own treasure chest filled with Aztec gold—though that did sound awesome—but everything else was definitely on my list. Mashimoto was stealing my dream, and I knew what was next on his long list of thievery. He was going to steal my friends. Wasn't it obvious?

There had to be something I could say that would just crush his ridiculous smile. Something so unexpected that Hi Mashimoto would simply fall to his knees and beg me for an ounce of my coolness.

Then an idea came to me, smacked me right between the eyes with enough force to almost cause me to tip over backwards. "Oh yeah? Well, guess what? My tree house has a TIME MACHINE!"

Have you ever had one of those moments in your life when you step out of your body and watch yourself about to say something pretty dumb? For a second you realize that if you go through with saying it, you'll end up causing soooo much trouble. But it doesn't matter—you can't stop yourself. I had one of those moments standing in front of Hi Mashimoto while Snow Cone caught brain freeze after eating a gallon of shaved ice.

Mashimoto's smile instantly shriveled. His hands trembled, and his golden jumpsuit twinkled like sparkling apple cider. Oh, I had stepped in something stinky.

"I don't believe you," he said. "You're lying."

"I don't lie," I lied. I rubbed my knuckles against my shirt. "So, you see, it doesn't matter what your tree house will have. It will never be as cool as mine. If I wanted, I could have a waterbed with fish and a telescope, but I don't need that junk. I have a time machine, and you can't beat that."

"Prove it!" Mashimoto demanded. "Take me to your tree house and show me."

I just shook my head. "Sorry, pal. My tree house is for members only, and I don't think you have a ticket." Ooh, that felt good.

Hi's golden jumpsuit started swelling up like a float in the Thanksgiving Day parade. I grabbed Snow Cone's arm and pulled him away.

"We're leaving?" Snow asked, shaking all over. He had just had a shaved ice binge, and his skin was an unhealthy shade of turquoise.

I didn't answer. Instead, I grabbed a tiny whistle from my pocket and played a little tune on it. Pigeon Criggle appeared from behind the bounce house. "Sir, reporting to duty!" Pigeon shouted, saluting. He was dressed like a chicken, which almost made sense.

"Pigeon, I need you to send this message to everyone in the club. Tell them *she'll be comin' round the mountain when she comes.*"

Pigeon looked around, panicked. "Who'll be coming around the mountain?" he whispered. "It's not Ms. Borfish is it?"

"Pigeon, what have I told you about the code?"

"Sorry, sir." Pigeon lowered his head, ashamed. With a final salute, he sped off, fluttering toward the other side of the yard.

I knew I didn't have much time to think of something to get me out of this mess. Mashimoto would come knocking, no doubt about that. And when he did, if I didn't have a time machine, or at least something that could pass as one, my reign at Pordunce as the kid with the coolest tree house was over.

Chapter 4
No Ordinary Outhouse

Back at the tree house, I waited for the complaining to end before I unleashed the bad news. I had a headache and so did Snow Cone, but his was self-inflicted from all the cartons of shaved ice he had eaten.

"Why did we have to leave so soon, Hashbrown?" Whiz griped. He was dripping from head to toe with pool water, and it was a slight shade of yellow. "That was the most fun I've ever had on a waterslide."

"That's because you've been banned from every water park this side of the Mississippi River," I answered.

"Uh, and he's technically banned from the actual Mississippi River as well," Hummus added.

"You're not helping, Hummus." Whiz huffed. "It isn't fair. I was having one of the greatest nights of my life and then he showed up quacking." Whiz glared over at Pigeon who was sitting in the corner, nibbling on wheat crackers.

"That wasn't quacking," Pigeon said, pecking at the crumbs on his shirt sleeve. "That was cawing . . . like a crow." He nodded. "Mr. Hashbrown always wants me to keep a low—"

"Oh, put a cork in it!" Whiz shouted. "Whatever it was, it was loud and annoying."

"Yeah, and some of us don't really know the meanings of the secret codes just yet," Butter Bibowski said. "I thought 'she'll be comin' round the mountain when she comes' meant that we were supposed to roll ourselves in a blanket and act like a burrito. Luckily, Four Hips showed up while I was looking for bean dip and explained what Pigeon was squawking about."

I tried not to smile, but the image of Butter tightly rolled up in a tortilla and covered in guacamole was almost too much to handle. "I know. I'm sorry," I said. "Look, guys, something big happened at Mashimoto's." I held out my hands to silence the crowd.

"Yeah, we know," Measles said. "But that's no reason to have us evacuate."

"You know?" I asked, my eyes growing wide. How could Measles know already? He wasn't around when I was talking with Mashimoto.

"Of course we know, but elephants are always doing that at the circus. That's why they have all those clowns running around with big scoopers."

Measles had drifted way off the subject, which was annoying but typical.

I shook my head. "Measles, did you take your medication?"

Measles blinked. "Take it where?" He popped a blister under his ear.

"Never mind. Snow Cone, do you want to help me out here?" I looked over at him for support.

"Help you out with what?" Snow Cone asked.

"Help me explain to everyone what I told Mashimoto."

Snow Cone shrugged his shoulders. "I don't know what

you're talking about. One second I was eating shaved ice while you and Hi were chatting about your tree houses, and the next second you've got everyone scattering."

I should've known better. Whenever Snow Cone starts eating shaved ice, he tunes out the rest of the world and goes into a trance. He once followed a shaved ice vendor onto a bus and was picked up three days later by the local authorities in downtown Manhattan. He had no idea how he got there or why he was carrying a paper sack filled with dung beetles.

"You didn't hear what I said?" I asked out of the corner of my mouth. I pulled Snow Cone to the side.

"Hear what?" he asked.

I sighed, looking cautiously around the room. "Snow Cone, *the heat is on in Saigon*." Thank goodness for the code. Whenever I was trying to not start a riot with my friends, I could rely on the secret code Snow and I created back in first grade.

Suddenly, Snow panicked. He shot his hand into his pocket and pulled out a tiny notebook containing all the definitions of our secret code language. After thumbing through a few pages, he literally shrieked. "Why did you say that?" he shouted. "Are you crazy? Where are we going to find a time machine?"

Everyone in the tree house jumped up from their chairs and started shouting at once. So much for not starting a riot.

"Settle down, everyone!" I shouted over the uproar.

Whiz started in on one of his patented rain dances while the new recruits avoided the puddles. Measles went cross-eyed for a solid minute. Four Hips started hallucinating and nearly ate Pigeon, and Snow Cone just shook his head in disappointment.

"Why, Hashbrown?" Snow Cone asked. "Why did you have to lie? It's not like anything Mashimoto says matters."

"Oh yeah?" I said, pointing my finger out the window. "We don't have any of that cool stuff. Mashimoto's gonna have a jet pack, and all we have is this beat-up tree house."

"How do you know he's gonna have a jet pack?" Whiz asked, looking at me eagerly. "Do you think he'll let us take turns flying it into town?"

"Whiz, can it!" I snapped. Whiz lowered his head in embarrassment. "Guys, we don't have to build a real time machine, we just need Mashimoto to think we have one. That's all."

"Why's that so important?" Four Hips asked, finishing off his carton of cream cheese frosting and starting in on Hummus' edible markers.

I gnawed on my lip. There was once a time when I had the coolest stuff. Back then, everyone wanted to see my reclining chair and mini fridge and everyone wanted to be in my club. Now Mashimoto was taking over my turf.

"You just don't get it, do you?" I asked. "We can't let him win! If he does, things won't be the same."

"But he already has all those cool things, and he's getting a new tree house too. Do you think just because we have a time machine that will make any difference to him?" Measles asked.

I nodded my head. "Oh, it will, all right. Mashimoto will think no matter what his new tree house has, it will always be second place to ours, especially if we have a time machine. He can't win," I repeated. "I have to win! I mean . . . er . . . we have to win."

Everyone mumbled under their breath. They were getting tired. It was late, practically past our bedtimes, and we had just spent a few hours gobbling nothing but junk food.

"His club's already growing bigger," I continued. "Everyone is joining him. They should be joining us." I darted over to the filing cabinet.

Snow Cone placed his hand on my shoulder. "You said yourself we were going to have to wait until next year before we added new members to our club. We just don't have the space."

"I know we don't have the space, but I still want to have the tree house and the club that everyone wants to join. I still want a sell-out crowd for our Spring Conference—don't you? Do you remember the time when kids would stand in line for days, camping out beneath the tree house ladder, waiting for a chance to hear your speech on how to build a snow ball catapult?"

Snow Cone smiled as he remembered. "Those were good times, but we have to let it go. There's going to be a day when kids no longer want to come hear our wisdom . . ."

I yanked a large roll of paper out of the filing cabinet and unrolled it so everyone could see. "If we build this . . . they will come!" I said triumphantly.

Everyone stared at what looked to be the blueprints of an—

"That's an outhouse, Hashbrown," Whiz said, breaking the silence.

I blinked several times and stared down at the paper. Whiz was always right when it came to bathroom stalls. To be honest, I had no idea what a blueprint of an outhouse was doing rolled up with the rest of our files, but it didn't matter. I was digging a hole, and I wasn't going to stop until I was buried in it.

"Good job, Whiz," I said. "Of course it's an outhouse, but not just any outhouse. This is our time machine."

"Hashbrown, pal." Snow Cone was running his fingers

through his hair. He did that whenever I started acting crazy. "You know you're my best friend, but you just said this was a picture of an outhouse. How can it be a time machine too?"

"Yeah," Whiz added, a mysterious tone rising in his voice. "Because I've had my theories about the same thing." He rubbed his hands together. "In fact, I'm pretty sure I saw Abraham Lincoln in one of the toilets at Camp Bugby, but I've never been able to prove it."

I groaned. "Not a real time machine, guys. A fake one. If we can build this, maybe we can fool Mashimoto into thinking it really is a time machine. All we need are some gizmos and gadgets. A few buttons here." I pointed to a couple of spots on the blueprint. "And maybe hook up a laser or two and who knows? We could totally pull this off."

"Where are we going to find supplies to use?" Bulkins asked. "We've already spent our entire budget."

"And none of us know how to build anything like that," Whiz said, hopping up and down on his toes. All this talk about outhouses was taking its toll on him. "How would we start?"

"Snow," I said, reaching down for my latest copy of the Pordunce Elementary year book. "Maybe I was wrong when I said we didn't have enough space. Maybe we'll have to add a few new members to our club, after all."

Chapter 5
A Very Hairy Criminal

The next morning, I sat in Ms. Pinken's science class drumming my hands nervously against my desktop. My eyes were glued to the back of Hi Mashimoto's head. I had to stay cool and keep an eye on him. While I sat there learning very little about science, my friends were sneaking around the hallways, completing a dangerous mission. We needed new recruits to pull off the miracle time machine, and we were looking for anyone wanting to join. Well, let me correct that. Not just anyone. We were looking for geniuses, brainiacs, and freaks of nature. Luckily Pordunce Elementary had quite a few of them enrolled. I didn't do this often. Snow Cone was right when he said we didn't have enough space for new recruits. We already had two members of the club that weighed so much the tree branches were starting to sag. But this was an emergency. Snow and the rest of the gang were skipping their second period classes to plaster the hallways with posters announcing open enrollment for the club.

"Hashbrown?" Ms. Pinken's high-pitched voice snapped me out of my trance. Apparently, she had called my name six times.

"Yes, Ms. Pinkens?" I asked, looking up at her and wiping the annoyed expression off my face.

"It's your turn," she said.

"My turn to what?" I asked as several classmates started to giggle.

"It's your turn to complete the formula." Ms. Pinkens waved at the chalkboard where a bunch of letters, dashes, and numbers were drawn. This was going to stink. I was awful in science. It was my worst subject by far.

"I . . . uh . . . would love to," I said. I rose from my desk and walked toward the front of the classroom.

As I brushed past Mashimoto's desk, he whispered. "Maybe you should go back in time and study a little harder."

The hair on the back of my neck stood on end. I didn't say anything. I was too busy concentrating on the chalkboard. Ms. Pinkens handed me her piece of chalk, and I stared up at the horrifying chalkboard trying to think back to some of the past lessons. I stood there for a solid minute, knowing the entire class was watching my every move. Closing my eyes, I snatched up the eraser and erased everything on the board.

Ms. Pinkens started stammering. "What on earth are you doing?"

I was trying to buy some time, but now the board was blank, and I couldn't remember what letters and numbers had been up there. This was humiliating. Mashimoto was watching me. He could see I was an idiot.

"Oh, sorry," I yelped. I picked up the chalk again and started drawing. I had almost completed a picture of a buffalo when Mr. Buse burst into the room, holding a long, broken piece of chain in his hand.

"What is it, Mr. Buse?" Ms. Pinkens asked in alarm.

Mr. Buse's eyes darted around the room. "Prudence!"

he barked. "Do you have anything thicker than this? I need something heavy duty."

"What for?" she asked, digging around in her desk drawer and pulling out a massive steel chain that was probably once used to fish for blue whales. I didn't even want to know why she had that thing stowed away in her desk.

"Come quickly. There's been an accident." Mr. Buse snatched the heavy chain from her hand and vanished from the room.

I looked at Ms. Pinkens, who seemed worried as she hurried out the door after him. Chucking the chalk, I charged after her as well. If there was an accident at Pordunce, I needed to know about it. As I ran out, I grabbed my notepad from my pocket and started scribbling. There was a strange feeling in the air—something terrible had happened.

I glanced down at my paper and read what I had written.

Prudence Pinkens.

That was too good to be true. You never know when that sort of information would come in handy for blackmail. With those initials though, it was no wonder she was Whiz's favorite teacher.

Out in the hallways, students stood with their backs against the lockers. Their faces were stretched in looks of horror as they stared down at the smashed trophy case next to Mr. Buse's classroom. Glass covered the floor, and Mr. Hackerbits, the nearly blind school janitor, was trying to sweep it up as best he could. So far, none of the glass had been touched, but several kids' backpacks had been swept into a massive pile with Pigeon perched nervously on top.

"What happened?" Ms. Pinkens covered her mouth in shock.

Mr. Buse was almost in tears as he scanned the trophies in

the case, searching for any damage. "There I was, standing in class, teaching my students about the American Revolution, when all of sudden there came this mighty crash." Mr. Buse's hands shot into the air for emphasis. "When I came out, this is what I found."

"Who could've done such a thing?" she asked, her eyes resting on me and glaring. Typical. She would suspect me even though I was clearly in her classroom, trying to draw a buffalo, when everything went down.

"Oh, I caught him all right. That's why I needed this chain here." Mr. Buse pointed over by the bulletin boards where Yeti Mckean sat with his hairy legs crossed and broken pieces of chain links littered on the ground. "His leg hair's unlike anything I've ever seen. Sawed right through my chain."

Yeti Mckean? He was one of my new recruits! What was he doing breaking into the trophy case? That wasn't his assignment. I quickly double-checked my notes from last night's meeting. There was nothing written in my notes telling Yeti to rob the trophy case.

I walked slowly over to Yeti. His head was bowed. "What are you doing?" I whispered. Yeti's head twitched, but he didn't answer.

"Stay back from him, Hashbrown!" Mr. Buse barked. "I haven't had a chance to frisk him, yet."

"Yeesh," I said, cringing. I looked down at Yeti in pity. Poor guy. A Mr. Buse frisking was right up there with going to the dentist after eating a beanbag filled with cotton candy. It wasn't pretty. Still, I couldn't understand it. We ran a background check on Yeti. As far as we could tell, he was clean. What made him suddenly go criminal?

"Well, did he steal anything?" Ms. Pinkens asked, stepping around the pile of backpacks and Pigeon to get a better look at the crime scene.

Mr. Buse frowned and plucked Yeti's backpack off the ground. Reaching his hand in, he pulled out a tiny silver cup, no bigger than a juice box. "Only this. It's not anything important. I ran a full inventory on all of the trophies, and as far as I can tell, everything else is still there." Mr. Buse had four dozen of his own trophies displayed in that case. Nothing made him more proud. As he handed the tiny cup over to Ms. Pinkens, I saw what the trophy was for. Second place in the all-county, left-handed marble shooting tournament. I had won that trophy when I was in second grade. It was the award that had started it all for me and my marble shooting career.

I blinked in shock. Why had Yeti tried to steal that trophy? A true friend would never do such a thing.

Mr. Buse scratched his chin and whistled. "It's a good thing for you that was the only thing you took," he said, pointing at Yeti. "If there had been just one scratch on any of my lacrosse trophies, I would've had you cleaned up in a different type of bath, my friend. One filled with hot wax."

Yeti shuddered and then passed out completely.

There was something strange about all this. Something unnatural. I didn't want to believe it. Yeti was a good guy—weird and hairy—but good. I had trusted him with access to my club, and this was how he repaid me?

As I stared down at Yeti, someone tapped me on my shoulder. I spun around, expecting to see Ms. Pinkens and jumped back in alarm. A very tall, strange-looking man stared down at me behind dark sunglasses. He had long flowing black hair that poured down over his ears and a bushy red moustache that looked like some hairy slug had crawled beneath his nose. He was wearing blue denim coveralls and muddy brown boots and then, oddly, he was also wearing a white laboratory coat.

"Excuse me, but what happened to that boy?" he mumbled.

"He had an accident," I said. "Who are you?" I tried to peer beneath his sunglasses.

"I'm here to fill the vending machines with soda pop." The man smiled awkwardly. I looked around for his cart of sodas but didn't see anything. The vending machines weren't even down this hallway.

"They're over there," I said, pointing behind him. The man never turned around, but kept his eyes, or at least his sunglasses, focused on me.

"Oh, I know where they are," he said. "Would you like to try one of our newest flavors?" He brought out an open can of pop from his coat pocket. It was a white can with a red streak around the middle. Some of the bright blue soda had spilled down the side.

I was thirsty, but that can was already open. I shook my head and sidestepped around him. He didn't turn, but continued to stare down at the spot where I had been standing. After a few moments, he wandered back the way he came, stopping for a second to examine the drinking fountains.

What a weirdo! Principal Herringtoe really needed to start screening who he allowed in and out of the school. I was a little bothered, but my thoughts immediately returned to Yeti. I whistled for Pigeon and glanced over my shoulder as he swan-dived off the pile of backpacks, landing gracefully in Mr. Hackerbit's mop bucket with a soft splash.

"You have a message for me, sir?" Pigeon asked, saluting as usual.

I nodded. "Find Snow Cone and tell him . . ." I hesitated. Someone was watching me. Spinning around, I noticed somebody at the end of the hall duck away from view. I wasn't able to get a good look at whoever it was.

"Pigeon, tell Snow everything is normal and to continue on with the plan."

"But, sir, Yeti's just robbed the trophy case!" Pigeon started flapping in a state of panic.

I reared back and slapped him across his face. "Get a handle on yourself!"

Pigeon looked stunned for a moment, but then relaxed. "Thank you, sir, I needed that."

"Everything's fine, Pigeon. We continue on with our plan like nothing happened." I then pulled in close and whispered in Pigeon's ear. "Also tell him this: *Only you can prevent forest fires.*"

"Only me, sir?" Pigeon asked hopefully.

I rolled my eyes.

"Oh, right, sir!" Pigeon saluted once more and shot off like a bottle rocket.

As I walked alone back to class, I kept my eyes peeled, searching for anyone that might be watching me. I needed time to think, and my buffalo drawing was waiting to be completed back in Ms. Pinkens' class. I needed to be on my guard and just pray my friend would carry out the rest of the plan without any trouble.

Chapter 6
Time to Dig up the Eggs

More strange things happened at school the rest of the day. Two more of my fellow students were caught doing crimes. Camo Phillips got nabbed sneaking into the lunch room during third period and trying to change all of the menus to Wednesday's lineup. I don't know how Ms. Borfish spotted him because he camouflaged himself to look just like a barrel of oatmeal. Camo was usually one of the good guys. Plus, hash browns were served on Wednesday. Why would he do that?

Teeter-totter Williams was the next to join the list of bizarre crimes. He went absolutely nuts during recess, nearly destroying the teeter-totters, which were his favorite thing to ride. He was on his way toward our marble hangout with one of the poles when Mr. Hemroin tackled him. He was a sixth grader, and we had never been close, but trying to destroy my marble arena was completely uncalled for.

During lunch, Snow Cone and I didn't speak much; we just ate our meals in silence. At each of the other lunch tables, it seemed there were students more interested in our conversation than their lunches. The school wasn't safe anymore. There were too many enemies. Too many spies. Luckily, we were able to avoid Mashimoto and his followers. Everything else with our plan went smoothly, and just before dinner time, we had quite the crowd gathered in my tree house.

"Could everyone please be seated?" Snow Cone spoke into a microphone on the podium. I bought the microphone a couple of weeks ago with my allowance, and although it wasn't a real microphone, just a toy with pink and gold buttons that would randomly sing the song *Princess Puppy Party*, it definitely got everyone's attention. Everyone became quiet all at once. Snow Cone cleared his throat. "As you may have already heard, one of our new recruits is no longer with us." A hush fell over the room. "Yeti Mckean has chosen a life of crime, and even worse, he's made a clear attack against our leader." Snow Cone looked at me, and I carefully turned to watch everyone in the room. Were there others here that would follow Yeti's lead? I had no way of knowing.

"Now, on to business," Snow Cone continued. "Because of Yeti's treachery, we actually have a couple of slots open in the club. Unfortunately, we will not be able to give each of you memberships to Hashbrown's club tonight."

Several of my classmates erupted with complaining.

"What do you mean by that?" shouted Echo Rodriguez. "What do you mean by that?" he echoed in a softer whisper. "You mean to tell me, I had to sit next to Gurgles the entire time and there's a chance I might not get in?" he griped.

Gurgles Dunderland's stomach made the sound of a dying lawn mower. "It's just gas," he said, clutching his belly.

"Everyone, please!" Snow Cone shouted into the microphone. "We're going to hold tryouts, and you will have to pass a couple of simple tests to see whether or not you'll make it in the club."

I felt a little guilty. After all, I had already picked who I wanted to join the night before, but I needed to make it look like it was a completely random choice. Especially if there could be spies in our midst. I wouldn't put it past Mashimoto to send someone to try out for my club. Luckily, there was really no chance for anyone to make it past our tests unless I let them. They were fool-proof.

Gurgles Dunderland and Squeaky Mittons had to sit for five minutes without making a single noise from any part of their body. They lasted thirty seconds, and we were forced to open the windows.

Wish Bone Parker and Echo Rodriguez had to guzzle a thirty-two ounce glass of Molten Cola while being dangled upside-down over the tree house ladder. My mom's petunias are now brown and wilted.

Fibber Mckenzie was given his usual lie-detector test. The poor guy had tried out at least a dozen times to join my club, and he always got stumped when we forced him to take the test.

Snow Cone glared at me as we strapped Fibber into the chair and attached the electric cords to his earlobes. "I can't believe you're going to make him do this again," he whispered under his breath.

I looked down at Fibber and sighed. He *was* a really cool guy. If it weren't for his lies, he would have been a member a long time ago. "All right, all right," I said. I decided to take it easy on him and told Fibber if he could tell the truth just once during his two minute test, we'd let him join.

"This is going to be easy," Fibber giggled. "I pass these things all the time when I'm working as a secret agent in New Zealand."

The Lie-Detector machine chirped.

"Okay, Fibber, here goes," Measles said, putting on some earphones and adjusting a knob on the machine. "What's your real name?"

Fibber smirked and waved his hand dismissively. "Come on. That's easy. Fibber Monrovia Mckenzie."

Chirp.

"Monrovia?" I asked, trying not to laugh. "All right, maybe we shouldn't be the ones asking the questions. Why don't you try telling us something true about yourself?"

Fibber shrugged. "Sure. My mom's got a pet kangaroo named Joshua."

Chirp.

"I have four thumbs."

Chirp.

"I was once locked up in an Irish prison for three months."

Chirp.

"I never have to pay for school lunch because I can gargle creamed corn."

Chirp.

I looked down at the report printing off the machine. "Has he told the truth yet?"

"What are you talking about?" Fibber raised an eyebrow. "I always tell the truth."

Chirp.

We helped Fibber out of the chair and patted him on the back. I glanced over at Snow Cone and shrugged as if to say that at least I tried.

"Well, maybe we'll try again next year, Fibber," Snow Cone said, showing Fibber to the exit.

"Yeah, maybe, as long as I'm back from my shark hunting expedition," Fibber said.

Even though he was no longer strapped to the Lie-Detector machine, it gave out one last *chirp* for good measure.

We whittled the rest of the group down in pretty much the same way. By the end of the night, we had made our selections. Gavin Glasses and Mensa Michaels sat cross-legged on the floor, laughing wildly at a calculator. I bit my lip. This wasn't going to be fun. Half the time, I never understood a word these two said, but I wasn't doing this for fun. It was all business. Gavin and Mensa were geniuses. The only reason why the two of them weren't working for the government cracking codes was because Gavin was planning on winning the state math tournament and Mensa was deathly afraid of carpet. If there was anyone at Pordunce Elementary that could help me convince Mashimoto we had a time machine, it was these guys.

"Congratulations!" I said, clapping my hands and nodding at the rest of my friends to do the same. "It was a close race, but you two are in. You're our new recruits."

"But we didn't have to do anything," Gavin said, adjusting his glasses.

"What does that matter?"

"It matters plenty," Mensa chimed in. "My great-grand-father always said that one is required to be tested in order to prove one's worth."

"Agreed," said Gavin. "We have not been tested. A true genius would never settle for handouts. We must prove our worth."

I winked at Snow Cone, who smiled and popped his knuckles. "All right. You want to prove your worth?" I handed Gavin the rolled up set of outhouse blueprints. "Here's your test."

★ ★ ★

Just before the sun rose the next morning, I looked down at the finished plans of my time machine. It had taken Gavin and Mensa all night to complete it, but now my blueprints no longer looked like an outhouse. Written in the margins was a list of all the items we would need to complete the project.

"You've done well," I said, patting them on their backs. "You're sure if we follow these instructions, we'll be able to travel back in time?"

Gavin Glasses clicked his tongue. "Now that's the question isn't it? From all of my studies, if you were able to find every one of these materials than yes, I suppose it could work."

I glanced at the list of materials and felt my throat tighten. It would be difficult to find plutonium at the local grocery store.

"But to be honest," Mensa continued. "It would take a miracle to find everything. For now, if you can build most of it, this should pass inspection."

I looked at the rest of my friends who were all yawning and scratching their heads in confusion. They were all going to be grounded for staying out so late on a school night, and I could sense their frustration.

"Do you think it could fool Mashimoto?" I demanded. That was the most important part. Sure, it would be really convenient to travel through time, but for now, I just needed the machine to help me beat Mashimoto.

"I suppose if you were to hire some actors to stand in as people from the past and if you had the right lighting, and maybe a curtain made of sterling silver," Gavin said.

"And some fancy mirrors," Mensa blurted.

"Oh, yes, and a smoke machine for effect," Gavin said, nodding. "Then, yes, theoretically, it might work."

I blinked several times. "Where am I going to find fancy mirrors?"

"Or a curtain made of sterling silver?" Measles asked.

"Why do we need a smoke machine?" Snow Cone added.

"And who's this Theo Reticly guy?" Four Hips whispered.

I knew this was going to be one of the most difficult projects my team had ever done, but at least, we had somewhere to start. We now had the plans, but it was going to take all of our free time and a ton of money to pull it off.

"It's not possible," Snow Cone said. "Smoke machine? Trained actors? I don't think it's in the budget." Everyone else in the room agreed.

I bit my lip hard and glared at my friends. "We're not giving up that easily."

"But Hashbrown, this will cost a fortune to build. We'll never find that kind of money." Snow Cone said.

"Oh, yes we will."

"Yeah, I guess if you wanted to dip into our . . ." His eyes widened. "You don't mean pulling out our life savings?"

I nodded enthusiastically.

"But that's for emergencies only or for a trip to Canada if we ever get our passports approved. Whatever comes first!" Bulkins shouted.

"This is an emergency," I fired back. "And I think it's time we dig up the eggs."

Five years ago, when my dad built my tree house, every one of my friends began saving up their allowances. We put all the money in six panty hose eggs and buried them under the tree house. There was a small fortune down there that we were saving for the right moment. In my opinion, this was the right moment.

"You've lost your mind," Whiz said, startling awake. He had been snuggled up with a rubber sheet for most of the evening. "We have to vote on what we use that money for. It's in the rule book."

"I don't care!" I snapped.

"But you wrote the rule book," Whiz said.

"Yeah, Hash," Snow Cone said. "We can't dig up the eggs for just anything. You've got to let this go. So what if Mashimoto wins? It's not important. We're still the coolest club in all of Pordunce, even if he does have the coolest tree house . . ." Snow Cone's voice sputtered to a stop. He had already said too much, and I think he knew it.

"No!" I shouted. "This is my tree house, and I started the club. Whiz was right; I wrote the rule book, which means I can change the rules if I want to, and that means the money is rightfully mine. I'll decide on how to use it, and I'm using it to buy all the materials we need for the tree house. It's time to dig up the eggs, and if you don't like it, then you all can leave!"

The tree house trembled from my voice. The wooden boards groaned as if the very nails holding them together would fall out and send us toppling to the ground below. Bubblegum and Measles exchanged looks of shock, but then their eyes narrowed. I could tell my threat had changed them. Whiz Peterson rung out his sheets onto the floor and glared at me. One by one, each of my friends left the tree house. Even Pigeon, who had always followed me around like a little lost puppy with feathers, left as well. He waddled down the ladder with his head burrowed beneath his arm. The only people left in my tree house were me and Snow Cone.

"Well, now you've done it," Snow Cone said, shaking his head in disbelief.

"What did I do?" I asked.

"They're your friends, Hashbrown. You can't treat them like that."

"Yeah, well, they'll come around when they see the time

machine." I started down the ladder with a shovel in my hand. Snow Cone watched me as I lowered to the ground. "Are you going to help me or just stand there?"

Snow Cone threw his hands up in defeat. "Fine, I'll help you."

We dug with our shovels until the bus arrived to take us to school. Snow Cone didn't say much to me, and that was okay. I knew I had made him really mad, but it didn't matter. All that mattered was the time machine—that would fix the mess I had made. I was covered in dirt and I was exhausted, but in my hands were six bulging eggs filled with money. Snow Cone left to go clean up for school, and I stumbled back into my bedroom and collapsed onto my bed. I needed to convince my mom to let me stay home from school so I could rest, but most important, I needed to get started on my shopping list.

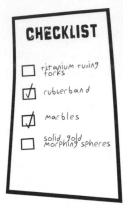

CHECKLIST

☐ titanium tuning forks
☑ rubberband
☑ marbles
☐ solid gold morphing spheres

Chapter 7
Bright Blue Turnips

The wheels of my shopping cart squeaked as I turned the corner onto one of the produce aisles at Marty Muffits Grocery Store. I thought this place had everything, but apparently it was running low on Titanium Tuning Forks, because I checked the silverware section, and there weren't any there. I stared down at my basket. It was almost completely empty. So far I had managed to find two items I needed on the list: rubber bands and marbles—and the marbles were not technically on the list.

Aargh! I hated shopping.

My mom joined me by the cart as I wheeled next to the shelves of fresh vegetables.

"Marbles, dear?" she asked me as she plopped a ten-pound bag of potatoes on top of my rubber bands. I shuddered. Potatoes were the key ingredient in hash browns. My mom could be so clueless at times. "Don't you already have enough marbles lying around the house?"

Just then an employee of Marty Muffits approached us.

He was a tall man with a long ponytail and what looked like a laboratory coat draped over his work uniform. He was also wearing dark-tinted sunglasses, which made look him oddly familiar, but I didn't know why. In one hand he was carrying a clipboard brimming with papers and in the other he held a spray bottle with bubbling blue liquid.

"Can I interest you in some of our delicious cauliflower?" the man asked. He began drenching the vegetables with his spray bottle.

"No, thank you," my mom said with a smile. "What's that you're spraying?" she asked politely.

The man stared down at the bottle as if it were his first time ever noticing it. "What this? It's vegetable food. They love it." He sprayed the blue liquid generously, covering every vegetable in sight.

"Sounds lovely," my mom said. "Come along, Hashbrown."

"I didn't know vegetables ate anything," I said, leaning in to examine a turnip that now looked like a blueberry.

The man leaned in next to me, pulling his clipboard close to his mouth, and whispered in my ear, "Oh, of course they do. Now, would you like to try one of those?" he asked.

"Uh . . . no," I said, backing away. I didn't eat turnips on my best days and now they were bright blue. I joined my mother, and we left the strange employee by the vegetable stand.

My mom handed me half of her shopping list. "Here, make yourself useful," she said. "I'm going to go get my nails done at the salon. Why don't you find everything I need, and I'll buy you a treat at the check stand."

"A treat? Really, Mom? Oh, goody," I said in my most sarcastic voice. Of course, I would take her up on the offer when I was finished—only a fool would pass up a free treat—

but I didn't want to appear too eager. Besides, I needed time by myself to go over my own shopping list. Something on my list had to be here, and I wouldn't have any luck looking for it with my mom hanging over my shoulder. I glanced at my list of materials. Solid gold morphing spheres? Sapphire-tipped locking bolts? A gallon of Yemen beaver wax? Maybe Marty Muffits wasn't the best choice for supplying my shopping needs. I folded the list and stuck it in my back pocket. There were still forty-two shopping aisles of exploring left, and I wasn't going to give up until I'd searched them all.

After fifteen minutes of wandering around only two aisles, I decided to give up. This was ridiculous! I doubted any of the items on the list really existed. Where was Snow Cone when I needed him? As if by magic, Snow Cone poked his head around the corner, nearly tripping over my shopping cart.

"Hey," he said.

"Hey," I answered. "What are you doing here?"

"My mom's getting her nails done."

I nodded. Didn't those women have anything better to do than get their nails sharpened?

"We saw your mom, and she said you were somewhere over here shopping," Snow Cone said, peering into my shopping cart and laughing when he saw what was in there. It was good to hear him laugh. I wanted to just give up, say I was sorry, throw away the shopping list, and forget all about Mashimoto, but I couldn't.

"Well," I said, pushing my shopping cart along. "Do you need anything?"

"No, I actually came here to tell you something else." Snow Cone looked over his shoulder. "I'm not going to help anymore with the time machine. I think it's a big mistake."

I could feel the shopping cart starting to quiver beneath

my hands. "Is that all? Do you have anything else to tell me?"

"Yeah, I do. Your mom wants you to pick up pickles; they're on aisle seven." Snow Cone took a step back as he could probably see my anger building.

"Oh yeah? Well, thanks for the info, but I don't need your help."

"Hashbrown," Snow Cone started to say, but I cut him off.

"No, that's it. I've had it! Don't bother stopping by the tree house anymore because you're not welcome!"

Snow Cone's eyes widened in shock. "You've gone wacko!" Turning on his heels, he stormed off, leaving me all by myself. We had never been apart for more than a day, and now I had banned him from our hangout. I wanted so badly to scream, and I probably would've had Hi Mashimoto not rounded the corner.

"Oh, sorry, Flinton, I didn't see you there," Mashimoto said.

Did he just call me *Flinton*? That was my real name, but no one called me by that name. It was downright disrespectful. I tried to push past him, but he stepped in front of my cart.

"I see you're out shopping. What for?"

"It's none of your business," I snapped.

"Well, we missed you in science today. It's a shame you weren't there to draw a cow on the chalkboard again."

"It was a buffalo, and I'm sure you really missed me." I looked behind him, trying to see who else of his little friends were hiding behind the magazine racks. "What do you want?"

"I was just wondering if I could stop by your place this evening and check out the time machine. I've been very excited to see it."

I felt my stomach bubble. "Uh . . . tonight's not a good night." I started backing my shopping cart down the aisle.

"Oh, come on, Hashbrown. Let's be friends." He pulled an apple from behind his back and handed it toward me. It must've been one of the fruits that weird employee had been spraying because it glistened with a bright blue liquid. "Here, why don't you have an apple? Then we could head back to your place and you could give me a tour."

"You're not invited," I said.

Mashimoto chuckled. "From what I hear, none of your friends are invited." He bowed slightly, and I took off down the other way. That was a low blow, but maybe I deserved it. Now I had no friends, and I wasn't even close to building the time machine. How was I going to do it? Maybe I had enough money, but money couldn't always buy plasma-converters.

Chapter 8
The Manatee's Gracious Gift

That next day at school, I walked the hallways alone. All of my ex-friends were hanging out at their lockers, laughing and joking about something—probably me. I didn't see Snow Cone, which was likely a good thing. This would be my first day of school where we didn't hang out at my locker right before first period. No one talked to me, not even Pigeon, who seemed to flutter in circles when he saw me, not knowing which direction he should go.

I felt awful. As I moped through the halls, not looking where I was going, I tripped over Luinda "The Manatee" Sharpie's folding chair. Luinda was a fourth grader that moonlighted as an amateur wrestler. She was pretty tough in the ring, but during the day she ran the school store out of a broom closet. She looked up from her store and hiccupped. She had been crying—that or someone had hit her in the face with a water balloon, but no one was that stupid.

"Oh, hi, Hashbrown," she whimpered. "Would you like to buy a mini-pencil sharpener? They're the hottest sellers right now. I have some in pink, butterfly-wing yellow, and I guess this is what they call—"

"I . . . I don't want to buy anything, Luinda," I said softly.

She stared at her sneakers and sniffed. Man, this was the first time I had ever seen Luinda cry. Usually, she was the one making grown men cry in the ring. What was going on?

"Are you all right?" I asked, glancing around at her store.

"I guess I'm f . . . f . . . f . . . f . . . fine!" Luinda let out a massive sneeze, spraying goo all over me. She buried her face in a handkerchief and started sobbing.

"Gee whiz!" I said, wiping my face clean of goo. "What's the matter?" It was weird to see her like this. She was The Manatee. She could do the figure-four death lock on most grown-ups.

"Oh, it's Hambone. I just don't understand him," she said, blowing her nose.

"Tell me about it." I nodded. "He's always mumbling. I think it's because he chews his tongue."

"That's not what I mean, Hashbrown," Luinda said. She pulled a long curl of matted hair from across her eyes and flicked it into place. "He's just so difficult to talk to."

I stared down at my shoes, thinking. "Have you tried grunting and pointing at sticks? I hear that's been known to work with him. He likes sticks, and Fibber told me Hambone can talk to pigs. There might be some truth to that."

"Hashbrown!" Luinda looked at me shocked. "That's not what I'm talking about." She seemed a little agitated, but I noticed she was starting to grin.

"What I meant is he's difficult to talk to because he doesn't listen to me no matter what I say."

I puffed out my cheeks. "Hm . . . Well, have you tried Q-tips? That's probably the reason he's hard of hearing. I've heard you can even use salt water, but just don't stand next to him when that stuff starts dripping out." I was pretty good at giving advice, and I was offering Luinda my best suggestions.

Luinda's face pulled back in a confused expression. "You're not helping me here," she said, but already her tears had dried up and she was starting to giggle.

"All I'm saying is you can't blame the poor guy for his wax build-up. It's a serious thing. Just ask Yankee Molicka. He uses a butter churn to clean his ears."

Luinda burst out laughing. "You're funny."

I half smiled. "Funny?" I asked. How was I funny? I was just trying to help, but she wasn't getting it. No wonder she and Hambone were having a love quarrel. This girl was dense.

"So, where are all your friends?" she asked, finally looking around and noticing I was all alone.

"They're not my friends anymore."

Luinda laughed even louder. From up close, I could practically see her tonsils vibrating like beach balls stuck above a box fan.

"No, I'm being serious," I said.

"Oh, I'm sorry." Luinda closed her mouth. "Why aren't you friends anymore?"

"We had a big fight over a really stupid thing, and now they all hate me."

"Even Snow Cone?" she asked. My head drooped even lower. Snow Cone used to be the boy of Luinda's dreams until Hambone came along. I could tell the very idea that Snow and I were no longer friends came as a shock to her. "What were you fighting about?"

For some reason, I decided to tell her everything. She was willing to listen, and I didn't have any other friends to talk to. When I finished, Luinda snapped one of her braces' rubber bands back into place.

"A time machine, eh?" she whispered.

"Yeah, silly, huh?" I wanted to laugh, but it was too painful. There never would be a time machine because I wasn't smart enough to make it.

Luinda opened her drawer and rummaged around for a second. There was no one else in the hallway because we had talked straight through the warning bell. I was going to be late to first period, but I didn't care. What was she pulling out of the drawer? Tightly folded into a perfect square and resting in the palm of her hand was a small piece of paper.

"Here," she said, holding out the object and dropping it in my hand. "Maybe this will help."

"What is it?" I asked, starting to unfold it. Luinda shook her head and swatted my hand away.

"Not here!" she hissed. Her head swiveled rapidly in either direction checking to see if the coast was clear. "Keep this a secret. It's a map."

"A map to where?" My heart was starting to thump in my chest.

"To the secret stairwell," she whispered.

"The secret stairwell?"

"SHHH!"

"Sorry. What are you talking about?"

"There's a secret stairwell here at Pordunce. It will lead you to a place that might have what you're looking for." Luinda started closing up shop. She emptied her display of erasable crayons into a small bucket and folded up her chair.

"Wait a second. I don't remember hearing about any secret stairwell here at Pordunce." My mind did a quick log of all the secret locations at the school.

"That's why it's a secret," she said, smiling.

"So this place may have a . . . time machine?"

Luinda batted her eyes innocently.

Could it be true? Could this be the answer to all of my problems? A feeling of excitement tingled in my fingers.

"Why are you helping me?" I asked.

"Because you make me laugh, and you've helped me realize Hambone's not all that bad."

"I did?" Okay, The Manatee had lost it. How did talking about earwax help her realize that? It didn't matter. What mattered was that I had a new chance to get things right. The sun was shining on me at that very moment. There was a chance that somewhere in the halls of Pordunce Elementary a secret stairwell lurked that could lead me to my destiny, and all I needed to do was wait until after school to find out.

Chapter 9
The Secret Stairwell

The halls were quiet, too quiet. It was as if the very building knew where I was going, and that was bad news. I could almost hear the walls whispering. "Hey look, mon. There goes that-a Hashbrown fella." Oh and by the way, when the halls at Pordunce Elementary School speak, they have a Jamaican accent. Thought you'd like to know. I nervously pulled Luinda's map out from my pants pocket and unfolded the page.

Peering over the map, I noticed the path led to the left down another hallway. I looked to my left, but found a solid wall. That couldn't be right. Aside from hundreds of fading blue bricks, there was nothing out of the ordinary. The map was wrong—or worse, it was just some kind of mean joke. I moaned with frustration and leaned my shoulder up against the wall. Immediately, I toppled through to the other side and stumbled down two steps of a hidden staircase.

What just happened? Looking back, I saw that what I had assumed was a wall was actually a curtain. Amazingly, someone had painted the other side of the curtain to look exactly like any ordinary wall. I got to my feet, dusted off my shirt, and stared down into the darkness of the stairwell. This was another first for me. I thought I knew every square inch of Pordunce Elementary. Not once in my five glorious years of attendance had anyone ever told me of the secret stairwell. What really bothered me was how Luinda knew so much. Maybe her little store was more like a barbershop where ancient secrets were exchanged. I shrugged my shoulders and stared down into the murk, wondering if I had the guts to do this. What would I find down there?

I reached into my backpack and pulled out my survival kit. Every kid needs a survival kit with the essentials. My survival kit just so happened to have a flashlight, a gas mask, a spool of trip wire, two bottle rockets, and a year's supply of wax lips. Yep, the essentials.

Clicking on my flashlight, I made my way down to the second level. The stone steps were crumbly and weak. One false move and who knows where I'd end up. Not wanting to find out, I tiptoed down the stairs as lightly as I could. Once at the bottom, I shone my flashlight across the dusty stone walls. *How old is Pordunce Elementary, anyways?* I wondered. I could faintly remember somebody mentioning it had been built in the eighties, but by the looks of the strange hieroglyphs and cave drawings, it had been around for centuries. One of the drawings showed several stick figures dancing around a fallen rhinoceros. Weird.

I followed the path for several minutes in dim silence until I came upon a fork in the road. The path to the left looked like it might have ended after a hundred feet or so. I had a bad feeling about that path. There was more to it than just a simple dead end—no doubt about it. Something told me it wasn't the way I needed to go and after taking a deep breath, I headed down the other path. Eventually, I came upon a lonely door with the words "Keep Out" written in blood, or at least red ink. What if I was about to make a terrible mistake by awaking some monster that had been peacefully sleeping down here all these years?

"Snap out of it, Hashbrown!" I ordered myself. This was my last option and maybe the only way I was going to win the battle with Mashimoto and get my pals back. I knocked on the door, my fist creating hollow thuds against the wood. I waited for someone to answer. After several minutes, I knocked again.

From behind the door, I heard a faint noise. I pressed my ear against the door and listened. Something was approaching. I barely had time to remove my ear from the wood when the door creaked open and there standing in the doorway was . . . a skeleton.

"Gaboosh!" I shouted, toppling to the floor and curling up in the fetal position. I started sucking my thumb and tried to recall a happy memory.

"What're you doing down here, boy?" The voice snapped me out of my memory, and I squinted up at the doorway. Turns out it wasn't a skeleton. It was just some skinny old man that made skeletons look like they needed to go on a diet. The old man was wearing blue jeans, a frilly white shirt, and tap shoes. "Well? What're you doing down here?" he repeated.

I tried to talk, but all my lips could muster was a rather embarrassing raspberry that splattered spit all over the old man's face.

"Who sent ya?" he demanded, wiping the spit out of his eyes and stomping on the ground, which made a very pleasant tapping sound. "Tell me quick, boy, before I . . ." he started coughing, and his chest heaved like a rickety birdcage.

"Uh . . . um . . . The Manatee sent me," I said, stepping back and shielding my face. Who was this guy? How long had he lived down here? And . . . what was with the tap dancing shoes?

The man's eyes lit up. "Luinda? She sent you here?"

I nodded. "You know Luinda?"

"Of course I do. She's my niece. Pretty thing, isn't she?"

"Yeah," I said, raising one eyebrow and trying my best to agree. Luinda? Pretty? Uh . . . no.

"Well, if she sent you here, then you must be a decent boy and in need of some assistance. Come on in then. I'll see if I can fix you up nice."

Fix me up nice? What was this old man talking about? I could turn back. There was still time.

"I've got some gum drops around here, if you'd like," he said, adjusting his coveralls. "They're a little old and perhaps a little sweaty, but that makes 'em moist."

"No thank you," I muttered, gagging a little.

"Suit yourself. My name's Marlow Tanner, but you can call me Twinkles. Follow me."

Twinkles. Now there's a nickname I wouldn't wish on my worst enemy. That was just plain sick and wrong.

I guess I must've realized how desperate the situation was. Any normal kid wouldn't even think of following Twinkles into his dingy, smelly room with his sweaty gum drops, but there I was, tagging along. It didn't take me but a few glances to notice all the bizarre decorations.

What was this place? There were jars of gunk balancing on tables everywhere. Some of them bubbled, while others held an assortment of weird objects floating around. Fingernails, marbles, baby pacifiers, bacon . . . you name it. Several dogs and cats tiptoed back and forth, and I saw at least two dozen hamsters rolling around in plastic balls.

"Don't touch anything unless you plan on buying it,"

Twinkles snapped, stroking his chin with his bony fingers.

"Buy it? Why would I want to buy any of this?" I almost started to laugh.

"Why else did you come down here to Twinkle's Pawnshop?" Twinkles plopped down in a rocking chair and plucked one of his hamsters off the floor. After cooing at it and petting the plastic ball, he rolled the hamster down the floor toward a set of bowling pins at the other end of the room. Luckily for the hamster, its ball curved away from the pins and rolled into a mound of pillows.

"Another gutter ball, blast it!" he shouted. "I keep forgetting to put in the bumpers."

"Mr. Twinkles?" I asked, interrupting. "Who do you usually sell this stuff to?"

Twinkles paused and scratched his head. "Hmmm, well I suppose my last steady customer was a fellow by the name of Gabriel Yucatan."

"The Oracle?" I shouted. "That must've been like seven years ago."

"Yep." Twinkles sighed and gazed off toward the wall. "That Yucatan boy used to buy all the good stuff."

A hamster ball rolled over my toe and out of reflex I kicked up my foot. The poor rodent shot through the air, landing in a dirty laundry hamper. I could hear it chattering as it tried to roll its ball through a mountain of dirty underwear.

"Now," Twinkles said, "why don't you tell me what it is you're looking for?"

I stared down at a glass jar filled with what looked like breath mints—only I was pretty sure they were some kind of teeth. "I don't know what I'm looking for," I said.

"Need new shoes?"

"Huh?" I said. "Uh . . . no."

"Diapers? Blow guns? Blowfish?" Twinkles's eyes widened with every word.

"No, I don't need any of those things," I said, raising my voice to cut him off. "I don't even have any money." I had left the panty hose eggs under my bed. Even if Twinkles did have something I needed, which I highly doubted, how was I supposed to pay for it?

"That doesn't matter. Let's just say I'll take care of you now and then one day I'll ask you to return the favor," Twinkles said.

"Well, what kind of favor?"

"Don't you go a-worrying about that. Now, what kind of trouble are you in?"

I told Twinkles all about Mashimoto and how I had yelled at all of my friends and had even driven Snow Cone away. I told him everything. Twinkles stared at me for a very long time.

"All right, I know just what you need." Twinkles hopped up from his chair and scurried over to a row of cabinets. After rummaging around in some boxes, he returned, holding a large, shiny ball-like thing. It was silver, with lots of buttons and knobs and a small handle on the top. "This, my friend, will solve all of your problems."

"Awesome," I said. "What is it?" He handed me the ball, and I held it in my hands for a moment.

"It doesn't have a name. But do you see that button right there?" Twinkles pointed to a bright orange button just beneath the handle. "You push that, and I guarantee all of your problems will fizzle away."

"What does it do?" I asked, feeling a trickle of excitement in my neck.

"I just told you!" he snapped.

I lifted the ball closer to my eyes and stared at all the

buttons. "Is this what I think it is?" My fingers were trembling with anticipation. I had expected it to be bigger. Shouldn't it look somewhat like an outhouse?

"Of course it is!"

All this time, this crazy old man had been hiding a time machine down in his pawnshop. "You're sure?" I asked, hesitating a little. It just didn't seem likely Twinkles could have something as amazing as a time machine. "Have you ever used it?"

"Just once," Twinkles said. "And that was enough for me."

"So I push this button right here?" My thumb rested on the orange button, and Twinkles gasped.

"Don't push it right now!" he shouted.

"Why not? When should I push it?"

"It's too dangerous to push it right now. You have to wait until the moment is right. When that happens, you'll know what to do. But remember, you have to have a crowd around to see you. Otherwise, no one will believe you," Twinkles said.

The old man had a point. I wanted the whole school to witness my discovery of time travel. "And you swear this will work?" I asked.

Twinkles gave a little tap dance, winked, and said, "Remember our deal." Then he pushed me through the doorway. "Now, get on out of here, so I can eat some dinner." And with one last double shuffle, he slammed the door.

At least now I understood how he got his nickname. I was standing in the dark hallway and holding what looked like a giant robot dropping. Things had just gotten interesting.

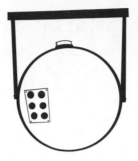

Chapter 10
Not Quite Time Travel

The next morning I learned there had been more incidents involving my classmates. Apparently, three other kids had been caught. Brandy Newspickle and Saddle Bags Bollinger had teamed up to break into Principal Herringtoe's costume closet. Mr. Coppercork found them trying to drop several pairs of gloves and some leather pants out the window to where Cup o' Noodle Hickok was waiting with a garbage bag.

Who were these people? Whatever their problem was, it didn't matter now. I wasn't going to let the craziness of my classmates ruin my perfect day of redemption. I walked through the halls with a little kick in my step. I patted the paper sack that held the mysterious silver ball. Now was not the time to reveal my secret weapon. I felt strongly about unleashing the device when the most possible students could see it, but when? Snow Cone walked past my locker, keeping his head low inside a magazine.

"Hey, Snow," I said, but he just hurried away. Just then, a piece of paper dislodged from the wall and fluttered down to the floor in front of me. It was an announcement from Principal Herringtoe. I smoothed out the wrinkles of the flyer and read:

Attention Students

Due to the recent crimes committed in our beloved hallways, there will be an all-school meeting today in the auditorium. Officer Killapup from the local police force will be giving a presentation. Each of you will have the privilege of being photographed and having your fingerprints taken. Some of the lucky ones will be given their very own computerized ankle bracelet to be worn at the school. Here's looking forward to a fun afternoon.

Also, I'm still looking for my collection of powdered wigs.

—Principal F. T. Herringtoe

Things were getting serious if the principal was inviting the local law enforcement to give a presentation. My eyes suddenly widened with excitement.

This was perfect!

Every kid in the school would be at the assembly. There would be no better opportunity to show off the time machine. It was as if some greater force was at work. Yes, sometime after lunch, everything would be back to the way it used to be. Snow Cone and I would be best of friends again, and Mashimoto's reign at the top of Cool Mountain would be over.

I stuffed the time machine in my backpack and darted off toward first period.

★ ★ ★

A few hours later, over six hundred kids sat cramped on the bleachers in the hot auditorium of Pordunce Elementary. Outside the sun was beaming down like a molten hot fireball from space . . . which is exactly what it is. All of the teachers sat in folding chairs in the center of the auditorium, glaring at us. I'm sure they were looking for the next criminal. Principal Herringtoe stood by a large podium and tapped the microphone with his finger.

"Okay, children, Officer Killapup will now start his presentation, and I want all of us to give our complete attention."

I glanced across the room, scanning each row for one of my friends and I almost yelped in shock. There, two sections away, were Whiz, Four Hips, Measles, and Bubblegum seated all in a row next to my mortal enemy, Mashimoto. Hi looked up from his handheld video game and gave me a friendly wave. He elbowed Whiz and pointed to me.

"How could you?" I mouthed. Whiz lowered his head in shame and most of the other kids on the row scooted away from him. I figured he must've whizzed. Mashimoto shrugged his shoulders innocently as if to say he didn't know why they were sitting by him, but I knew he was guilty. I watched as Mashimoto dipped into his backpack and pulled out several cans of soda. It was that new stuff the weird vending machine guy had tried to give me. Even from where I was sitting I could see the bright blue soda frothing at their lips. Of course, Mashimoto would have a whole bag of the newest and coolest soda pop.

Sitting a couple rows behind him and trying to avoid eye contact with me was Snow Cone. The traitor. Even if he wasn't sitting in Mashimoto's row, he was still within shouting distance. Mashimoto followed my eyes and looked over his shoulder at Snow Cone. He offered Snow a soda, but Snow Cone shook his head. I wanted to end it right then and there while the officer was gabbing about nonsense. I gritted my teeth and tried to control myself. I needed to stay calm, but I couldn't pull my eyes away from Mashimoto. Smiling, he took a small whistle from his back pocket and blew a single note. Instantly, Pigeon appeared floating next to him and waited for his command.

Oh, that was it! He had gone too far. I stood up from my seat.

"Yes, thank you," Officer Killapup said, shielding his eyes as he stared up at me. "Thank you for volunteering." He nodded toward me, and I looked around, confused. Apparently, Officer Killapup had just asked for a student volunteer. Suddenly, I realized this was my opportunity to show the school who really ruled the hallways. I grabbed my backpack and tromped down to the floor.

Officer Killapup rested his hands on my shoulders. "Now what is your name, little boy?" he asked.

"Hashbrown," I mumbled.

"Ah, yes. Trash Clown, is it?" Officer Killapup smiled to the audience, and everyone started to laugh.

"I said *Hashbrown!*" I snapped. My cheeks flushed purple.

"Pardon me?" Officer Killapup cupped a hand over his ear and leaned in closer. "What did you say?"

I threw my head back and groaned as the laughter grew louder and louder. This was humiliating. I would never be able to win my friends back standing there like a moron. I cradled my backpack in my arms and hugged it tightly against my chest.

"My, oh my. What have you got in there, Trash Clown?" Officer Killapup asked reaching for my backpack.

I pulled it back and glared at the officer. "Do you want me to show you?" I asked, feeling the anxiety growing in my throat. I unzipped my backpack and removed the shining silver ball in all its glory. I held it up in my hands for the whole auditorium to see. Officer Killapup cautiously stepped away from me.

"What is that?" he asked, glancing over at Principal Herringtoe with alarm.

"What this?" I asked, raising the ball even higher in the air to build the excitement. "This just so happens to be a . . . time machine!"

The auditorium exploded with sounds. My eyes darted toward my friends. They had risen from their seats and were standing with looks of awe on their faces. I knew what was going through their minds at that very moment. *Hashbrown's done it! He pulled it off.* I was their hero!

Beaming from ear to ear, I glanced over at Mashimoto who had also stood from his seat. Wisps of smoke rose up from his hands—he had literally crumpled his handheld gaming device.

"How do we know you aren't lying?" Mashimoto's voice rose above the uproar. All of the sounds ceased immediately.

"Lying?" I asked. "You think I'm lying?"

"Yeah, Hashbrown, lying," Mashimoto said. Everyone started talking again, only this time they weren't as excited as they had been when I first revealed the time machine. They didn't believe me. I saw Snow Cone standing in the bleachers. He looked disappointed. None of that mattered, though, because I had the secret weapon.

"I guess you're right," I said. "I guess I could be lying." My voice echoed through the auditorium. "There's only one way to find out." I rotated the silver ball in my hands, my thumb hovering above the orange button. It was my moment to prove it to the entire school. For a second, I paused. A feeling of dread passed through me. What if it wouldn't work? This would be a pretty inconvenient time to discover the time machine was a dud.

"You'd better work," I whispered to the contraption.

"Get going, Hashbrown!" a voice shouted from somewhere in the crowd.

"Yeah, go ahead and push the button!" Echo Rodriguez

screamed. "Push the button!" he repeated.

If they wanted a show, I would give it to them. Closing my eyes, I brought my thumb down hard. There was a click as the button lowered into the silver ball. At that exact moment all the students and teachers held their breath collectively.

But nothing happened.

I waited for a solid minute before I opened my eyes, praying I would be looking into the snout of a wooly mammoth and not at a student-filled auditorium. My shoulders dropped. I was still there at Pordunce Elementary, and everyone was starting to laugh again. Why hadn't it worked? Had I pushed the wrong button?

"Nice try, Trash Clown," Mashimoto announced to the entire student body. More snickering erupted. I was so angry I punched the silver ball with all my strength.

Then something finally happened.

The silver ball started hissing. It was quiet at first, but the hissing grew louder. That wasn't all—the ball started vibrating. One of the brightly colored buttons glowed green. This was it! Twinkles had been right all along. I was about to go back in time.

The sides of the silver ball started to pull apart as a loud grumbling noise and an off-yellow light poured out from the opening. I braced myself for whatever was about to happen. My heart was racing. My head was throbbing from excitement. I was sweating. The silver ball was . . .

Stinking!

It was probably just old. It had been cooped up in Twinkle's pawnshop for who knows how long. This was probably just a typical smell that . . .

Holy cow, it stunk something awful!

Clouds of green stench billowed out of the time machine. Thick, foul-smelling smoke formed a giant cyclone and started raging through the auditorium. I dropped the silver ball to the ground and covered my nose. Was this what was supposed to happen? I looked around the room. Everyone was gagging and trying to hold his breath. I had never smelled anything so awful in my entire life, and the fog of stench kept pouring out of the ball. Within seconds, I couldn't even see two feet in front of me. The fire alarm went off, and water from the sprinklers showered down on top of the student body. Instead of dousing the smoke, the water mixed with the green cyclone, turning it to the consistency of murky soup. I gaped in horror as six hundred students and a handful of faculty members fell to the floor, writhing in agony and completely covered in slop.

Stumbling away from the podium, I tripped over someone lying on the ground. It was Mr. Buse, and he was pinching his nose so tightly it had almost turned inside out.

"Hceshbreen! Weet hecve oo deen?" he squealed.

That's when everyone started to throw up. There was coughing, gagging, retching, and quite a bit of crying going on in the auditorium. Where was my gas mask when I needed it? I raced for the exit and had to hurdle over several other teachers as they crawled away from the podium.

Finally, the gas stopped pouring out of the silver ball, but it was too late. The damage had been done, and the stinky green soup was starting to flow down the halls of Pordunce.

Instead of beating Mashimoto and gaining my friends back, I had done something much worse. I would go down in history as the guy who set off the worst stink bomb the world had ever known, and there were over six hundred witnesses who could prove my guilt.

No doubt about it, I was in for a world of punishment.

Chapter 11
Pordatraz

It took twenty firemen, three fully-loaded fire trucks, and one million gallons of tomato juice to completely rid the school of the stench. The supposed silver time machine had been confiscated for evidence. I was pretty sure Twinkles had just pulled one of the biggest practical jokes ever.

The walls were a mixture of dull green and a sickening shade of red. Everyone's clothes smelled like dirty diapers. If there was any chance I had even one friend left at Pordunce Elementary, it had all gone up in a cloud of poop smoke that afternoon. I sat outside Principal Herringtoe's office, awaiting my trial. Would I be given a lawyer? A free phone call?

The door opened, and Principal Herringtoe appeared. From behind him, a tall man appeared and made his way through the door. He was bald and wearing a very familiar-looking white laboratory jacket. I figured it must be the new style or something—everyone seemed to be wearing them.

"Thanks again for coming in on such short notice," Principal Herringtoe said, shaking the man's hand. "That stink bomb really got my stomach churning, and I needed something to dull the pain."

"Of course," the man said. "Remember, drink all of that

medicine, and you'll be good as new." The man pointed to a small bottle of blue medicine in the principal's hand. Then he gave a slight wave and scuttled away.

"Who was that?" I asked, watching the man's white laboratory coat swish back and forth as he walked down the hallway.

"If you must know, it was my doctor. Well, not my regular doctor, really, but just one that does school visits. My stomach is quite messed up thanks to you." In his hand, Principal Herringtoe held my case file, which was about six inches thick. "Step inside, Flinton," he ordered.

I followed him into the office and sat down across from his desk.

"Hashbrown, Hashbrown, Hashbrown," Principal Herringtoe said after several long minutes of silence. "It doesn't look good." He folded his fingers over my file and shook his head.

"But, sir, it was an accident. I didn't mean to stink up the school. It wasn't my fault." Those were all really good arguments. It really was an accident. And it wasn't *all* my fault.

"Sure." Principal Herringtoe smiled. "Do you want to know what Yeti Mckean said after we caught him destroying the trophy case?"

"Uh . . ."

"Do you want to know what Brandy Newspickle and our friend Saddle Bags said when we stopped them from running off with my personal belongings?" Principal Herringtoe continued before I could say anything. "They said the exact same thing as you did just now. 'It wasn't my fault.'"

Oh, I was busted. There was nothing I could say that could clear my name, especially if I didn't want to sound any crazier than I already did. I lowered my head in shame. Now I was being compared to all those other kids who had run amok throughout the school. This was different. I had known exactly what I was doing. I'd been trying to beat Mashimoto.

"I'm sorry, Hashbrown, but you've left me with no other choice."

"What are you saying?" I asked, clutching my chair as tight as I could.

"I hereby sentence you to four weeks of hard time in Pordatraz Prison."

My hand shot to my heart. I felt faint. "Not that," I whimpered. "Anything but that!"

"I'm afraid so, Hashbrown." Principal Herringtoe closed my file and slammed a gavel against the desk. Court was adjourned; my case was closed.

★ ★ ★

The playground at Pordunce is rather large. There are swing sets, slides, and at least a dozen other unsafe and broken playground attractions. Despite nearly being condemned by the state, the playground is a place to go and get away from school and learning.

Now on the hill directly behind the playground, surrounded by high stone walls, stands Pordatraz Prison. It's old and weathered. Over the years, rain has faded the walls and rusted the black steel bars of the prison cells. It looks like an old, abandoned shopping mall, but with more guard towers and razor wire.

A prison, you ask? How can there be a prison that close to a school where young, innocent children frolic? Well, this isn't your normal, everyday prison. This is a recess prison—a fortress where the extremely naughty students are sent to be punished.

This was awful! How could I be sent to Pordatraz? I was

a good boy. Sure, I had done my share of punishment-worthy crimes at Pordunce, but so far nothing had ever landed me in Pordatraz. That was where the worst criminals could be found. That was where hard time really happened.

I felt like a fish out of water as we passed the rows and rows of cold metal bars. Principal Herringtoe led me through the entry gate and through a door where Ms. Borfish stood waiting. This was not good. Ms. Borfish worked in the cafeteria at Pordunce. She liked to call herself the school chef, but "School Troll" was a more fitting title. Everyone wondered where Ms. Borfish went after serving us our slop, and now I knew. She was the prison's warden.

There she stood, still wearing a hair net, but now she was also smacking a billy club against her palm.

"Well, well, well." Her lips pulled into a grin, and I saw her nearly toothless gums begin to grind against each other. This had to be the happiest moment of her life. She couldn't stand me. Maybe it was because I hated hash browns, or maybe it was because I once filled the milk cooler up with sardines. No one knew for sure. But whatever the reason, Ms. Borfish scowled whenever I appeared in the lunchroom and whispered the words "One day, Hashbrown!" under her breath whenever I walked past her.

"Ms. Borfish," I said with a gulp. "So nice to see you." I wanted to scream. I reached for my backpack—hoping to find a stray horsewhip in my survival kit—but there was nothing on my back. All of my possessions had been confiscated.

"Now, now, Ms. Borfish," Principal Herringtoe said, pulling me back out of her clutches, "no biting." Ms. Borfish's stomach heaved as she tried to control her breathing. She was going to have a wonderful time.

"Don't worry, Filbert. I'll take good care of little Hashbrown here."

Principal Herringtoe seemed relieved to be rid of me. After dusting off his suit coat, he tousled my hair. "Think cheerful thoughts," he whispered as he backed away from me. "You'll be out of here in no time."

Ms. Borfish cackled with glee as she dragged me through the hallways, passing hundreds of prison cells. Some of the prisoners' hands shot through the bars, trying to grab hold of my shirt, but Ms. Borfish kept them at bay with a cattle prod. These kids were the toughest criminals ever to walk the grounds of Pordunce. Some of them had spent their entire elementary careers locked behind bars. They were guilty of crimes I didn't even want to think about—stuff that could give me nightmares.

Finally, we arrived at my prison cell, which was already occupied by six other prisoners wearing grey jumpsuits and red do-rags on their heads. Their eyes glowed with delight when they saw me standing in the doorway. I looked around the room, hoping to find a friendly face, but I found nothing but cruel stares.

"There you go, Hash!" Ms. Borfish said patting my shoulders. "Nice and comfy. Maybe if you're good, I'll bring you by a little snack later on. How does a steamy plate of hash browns sound right now?"

"Hmmm, lovely," I whimpered. Ms. Borfish slammed the cell door closed and left.

I hadn't even had a chance to say good-bye to my mom and dad. Somewhere out there beyond those cold stone walls, they were probably wondering what had happened to their little boy.

"Well, look what we have here, boys," a really tough-looking kid with scars all over his face and a black patch over his left eye growled. He pushed up from the ground and walked over to me.

"Oh boy, this one's fresh out of school, isn't he now?" said another kid, curling a dumbbell in his massive hand.

"Hey, guys," I said, my voice sounding more like a squeaky toy. "Nice place you got here."

"You hear that, boys?" the first kid asked, sizing me up from head to toe. "This kid says he likes our place."

I needed a plan, and I was fresh out of them. My last few plans had been total stinkers . . . literally. What were they planning on doing to me? Was I going to be their punching bag?

"So how long have you been in here?" I asked the nearest kid. He had a round stomach and a big throbbing red nose. Out in the real world, I would've asked him for a Christmas present, but I wasn't about to say that to him in here.

"Me? I've been in for six months," the kid said proudly.

Six months? That was a lifetime.

"Ah, that ain't nothing," said the first boy, who must've been some sort of a ringleader. "I'm going on one year, and Frankie Folds over there—he's been here even longer." He pointed to the corner to where a skinny kid with long legs stood propped against the wall.

"How long?" I asked, trying to get their minds off of pounding me.

"Who, Frankie? He doesn't even remember anymore."

I noticed that behind Frankie Folds were hundreds of tick marks scratched into the wall. "What did he do?"

"We don't talk about our crimes in here," said a short kid with thick-rimmed glasses and a black crow perched on his shoulder.

"Why not?" I asked. The short kid looked to the ringleader, not knowing how to answer. The others looked over at Frankie Folds, who hadn't moved from his spot against the wall.

"Tell him," Frankie Folds said.

The short kid took a deep breath and nodded. "He's the reason Mr. Buse had a moustache for school yearbook pictures two years ago."

I waited for a second and then blinked. "That's it?" I remembered seeing that picture and having quite the laugh at Mr. Buse, but that didn't seem worthy of being locked up in Pordatraz. "Kids draw on their teachers' pictures all the time," I said. "That's nothing new."

Frankie smiled. "I drew it on Mr. Buse while he was posing for the picture," he said with a grunt. The other prisoners cheered.

Never mind. Frankie Folds was tough. I laughed and cheered with them. It seemed like the right thing to do at the moment.

"How about you?" I asked the ringleader.

He pointed at himself and curled his lower lip. "Back in the day my name used to be Salami Johnson." He smiled with the memory. "But now they just call me Frosty John."

Frosty John? *The* Frosty John? I had definitely heard about him. His crime was legendary. Last Christmas, Frosty John was caught after he rolled up seven giant snowmen out in the middle of the school parking lot, blocking all of the school buses. School had been cancelled for two days.

"You're Frosty John?" I asked in utter amazement.

"The one and only," he answered.

These guys were the real deal. I soon found out that at least one of them was responsible for every cancelled school day I had experienced at Pordunce Elementary. There was Salisbury Dickory, who simultaneously overflowed all the toilets six months ago, and even Wombat Willie from Australia, who built a fort in the cafeteria out of lunch trays and wouldn't come out for three weeks. They had to use tear gas to force him out. These guys were in all of the newspapers. Teachers spat whenever they said their names.

"How about you?" Frosty John asked, jutting his finger at me. "What did you do to get put in here?"

"Uh . . . it was really nothing," I whimpered. "It wasn't really my fault."

All of the kids in the slammer groaned pathetically. "Come on, you sissy! Tell us what you did!"

"Oh, I just set off a stink bomb in the auditorium today. That's all." I shook my head and looked down at my shoelaces. It was pathetic really. Just a puny little stink bomb.

"That was you?" Salisbury asked, his mouth hanging open.

"No way." Frosty John looked completely impressed. "We all saw the commotion even from here. The fire trucks. The bright green stink cloud." All the other kids patted me on the back. "Not bad. Not bad at all. I guess you're tougher than we thought."

Tougher? Yeah right. But at least I had them fooled. Maybe I *would* survive my four weeks.

"What's it like on the outside?" the short kid with the crow on his shoulder asked. The other kids called him Tyson the Teapot.

I shook my head. "What do you mean?"

"It's been so long since we've seen the playground. I just want to know if it's changed or not. I don't think I'd recognize it anymore." Several other kids mumbled in agreement.

"There's not much to do there. Play marbles or roll around in the sandbox, I guess."

"There's a sandbox now?" Tyson looked ready to cry.

I felt terrible for them. Sure, they had done the crime, but to not see the playground for months? That was just cruel and unusual punishment.

"What's it like with Ms. Borfish always around?" I asked.

"Oh, she's harmless. In about an hour, she'll head back to her trailer behind the school and watch cartoon reruns until she passes out on her couch," Salisbury said.

"Yeah, this place ain't so bad," Frosty said. "It's been getting a little crowded lately with all the new prisoners, but otherwise it's all right."

"New prisoners?" I asked. "You mean other than me?"

"Sure," said Frosty. "We've had all sorts of new inmates locked up recently."

I remembered the strange things happening in the school. Good kids turning bad and doing weird crimes.

"Those kids don't seem like the criminal type," Frankie said. "They definitely don't belong in here. What do you think's been going on?"

I didn't have an answer because I didn't know myself.

"We tried asking that one, but he doesn't want to talk to us." Frosty John pointed over to the sink. Lying down beneath it was a boy with a black fuzzy blanket covering his legs. At least that was what I thought until I noticed there was no blanket.

"Yeti?" I asked, pushing through the crowd and hurrying over to where Yeti was mumbling to himself. I bent down next to him. "What's going on?" I tried to get his attention, but he wouldn't look at me.

"He's been like that ever since they brought him in here," Tyson said.

"What's he been saying?" I asked, looking up at Frosty John.

Just then Yeti started talking more clearly. "Oh, okay, if you say . . ." he trailed off.

I held my breath as I listened.

"I'd love to try some new soda pop. It looks yummy."
Yeti.

"New soda?" Where had I heard that before?

"That's what he's been saying this whole time," Frosty
John said, shrugging his shoulders.

My mind raced, and suddenly I remembered the strange
vending machine guy who had offered me some new soda.
It was around the same time Yeti got caught for breaking the
trophy case.

"He's not the only one," Frankie said. "You ever hear of
a kid called Saddle Bags?"

"Yeah, I know him," I said.

"When Ms. Borfish brought him back, he was mumbling about eating some blue apple."

I jumped up in alarm. If there had been a piano player
anywhere nearby, I would've heard sinister music echoing
through the prison cell. Blue apple? Hi Mashimoto had tried
to give me an apple the other day at the store. An apple
covered in blue spray. Come to think of it, the soda had
been blue as well. Then I remembered how Mashimoto had
been handing out cans of that mysterious soda to all of my
friends at the school assembly. Was there some connection
between Mashimoto, that vending machine guy, and the
weird Marty Muffit's employee who was spraying blue stuff
all over the place? My mind clouded as I tried to think. Since
Mashimoto's big party in his backyard, my classmates had
started going crazy. Were Saddle Bags Bollinger and Yeti
Mckean just innocent victims?

Springing to my feet, I grabbed Frosty John by the shoulders. "I've got to get out of here!" I ran to the window and
strained to look through the bars. Outside, the wind was
blowing, but I could still hear the sounds of my classmates
playing on the playground.

"What do you mean?" Frosty asked. "You can't get out of here."

"I have to save my friends. I think Hi Mashimoto is behind these crimes, and if I don't stop him, he might try to take over the whole school!" It was all starting to make sense now.

"You don't get it, do you? You can't break out of here. We're on lockdown," Salisbury said. "You're just going to have to wait until your time is up like everyone else."

"I can't wait." I shook the bars with all my strength. "Please. There must be something I can do." I rested my head against the wall.

"Hashbrown, it's not so bad in here," Tyson said, patting me on the shoulder. "The food's a little stale, but they feed us pretty good."

I shook my head. "It's not that. It's just . . . wait, you guys get to eat during recess?" None of us other kids got to eat during recess.

"Yeah, do you want a bite?" Tyson handed me a crusty peanut butter and jelly sandwich. It looked old. I wasn't hungry, but it didn't matter because before I could even consider taking a bite, the black crow on Tyson's shoulder swooped over and gobbled up the sandwich in its beak. I barely had enough time to snatch my hand away before it was bitten.

"Grover!" Tyson scolded. "He's always doing that."

"What's with the bird, anyways?" I looked around. No one else had pets.

"Oh, he's just my little friend. He sings to me, and I'm trying to teach him to play checkers, but we have to use crackers. He loves crackers. And he's great at sending messages, too. Aren't you, little Grover?" Tyson patted Grover on his black-feathered skull.

"Messages?" I asked with a smile. A light went on in my head.

"Yeah, you know like a carrier—"

"Pigeon!" I shouted, cutting Tyson off mid-sentence.

Why hadn't I thought about it before? Pigeon Criggle always carried my messages for me. Would he still do it now? Even after I had kicked him out of my tree house? It was a long shot, but it was the only choice I had. If I could get him to send just one message, I might be able to make things right. I dug into my pockets and fished out my whistle. The rest of the kids watched as I blew hard on the mouth piece.

Seconds later, there was a loud crack against the cell wall, and the smell of Vienna sausages filled the air.

"Ouch!" Pigeon's tiny head poked up from beneath the ledge, and he peered into the cell through the bars. "Reporting to duty, Mr. Moto, sir!"

I took a deep breath and stepped into view of my former friend. "Hey, Pigeon," I said.

"Oh." Pigeon moved away from the bars. "It's you. I'm not supposed to talk to you. Mr. Moto says—"

"I know, Pigeon, but I have a favor to ask of you."

Pigeon stuck his fingers in his ears. "Can't talk to you." He started whistling.

"Pigeon, you have to listen to me. I know I've been acting crazy lately, but this is different. I treated you badly and I'm sorry. Hopefully you'll forgive me one day, but there's something else. Everyone at Pordunce is in big trouble, and I'm the only one that can save you."

"Not listening." Pigeon rocked back and forth on his heals, but his lips were beginning to tremble. I could tell I was getting to him.

"I know you're listening, and I feel bad asking you for a

favor, especially after all I did, but if you don't do this, something terrible is going to happen."

For just a second, I saw a gleam in Pigeon's eyes. He was about to crack under the pressure, but then his face grew cold. "You told us to leave," he said. "You don't need our help. That's why Mashimoto's our friend now." Pigeon looked away.

I tilted my head back and closed my eyes. This was not how I wanted it to go, but Pigeon was being stubborn.

"I'm sorry, Mr. Brown," Pigeon continued, "but Mr. Moto specifically said—"

"Pigeon, if you don't listen to me, I'm going to buy your mother a cat!"

There. I had said it. Pigeon's lips fell open. Several white feathers fluttered off his body. I knew he wanted to leave, but I also knew he was deathly afraid of cats.

"Fine," Pigeon sputtered. "I'll do you a favor. Just this once."

"Okay, listen up. I need you to send a message for me." I rubbed my hands together.

Pigeon's hands fell limply at his sides. "And what message do you want me to send to Mr. Snow Cone?" He leaned his ear closer to the bars.

"Oh no, Pigeon. I don't want you to send it to Snow Cone. There's somebody else."

Pigeon looked confused. "Somebody else? But who?" I whispered in Pigeon's ear, and his mouth fell open even wider. "Uh . . . are you . . . sure?"

"I'm positive. Now hurry."

Reluctantly, Pigeon shot away from the prison in a white blur.

Chapter 12
A Cotton Swab and a Plan

I had waited almost two hours with no sign of anyone coming toward the prison bars. All the kids had gone home for the day, and I was still stuck in the cell. I kind of wondered how this whole recess prison was even legal, but I guessed Pordunce Elementary did things a little different than most schools.

I tried playing checkers with Tyson and his pet crow to pass the time, but that was pointless. Every time I had a double jump, Grover would hobble over and eat my game pieces right off the board.

"He's so good, isn't he?" Tyson asked, stroking the crow's grimy feathers. "He never loses."

"That's because he eats all of your pieces!" I shouted. I was so frustrated, and the waiting was killing me.

Suddenly, the sky went dark as a black shadow fell across the checker board.

"What do you want?" Hambone Oxcart's deep baritone voice boomed from outside. Tiny bumps rose up on my arms and shoulders.

He was here! Pigeon had delivered the message! I slowly turned in my chair and faced the giant. He didn't look so good. His five o'clock shadow was now a full beard, and it looked like there were cobwebs dangling from the whiskers. Dark bags sagged beneath his eyes. The poor monster obviously hadn't slept much since breaking up with Luinda.

"Hi, Hambone, good to see you." My voice cracked. Was it really good to see him? I guess I would find out in a few short minutes.

"Get on with it, punk," Hambone growled. "You interrupted my snack. I hate when I'm not eating."

Oh boy, here goes."Hambone, I need your help."

"Yeah, I got that from the little birdy boy. Why would I help you?"

I then rattled off my sad, pathetic story. " . . . and if I don't get out of here and stop Mashimoto," I continued, "everyone at Pordunce could become mindless zombies."

Hambone stared at me for what seemed like forever. He looked confused. "Uh, zombies? Like this?" He held his hands out in front of him and dropped his head to one side, trying to mimic a zombie.

"Yes, exactly."

"Hmmm." Hambone picked a stray whisker from his chin. "So what?"

My heart pounded in my chest. "So, I have to stop him. You're my only way out of here."

Hambone chuckled. "What's in it for me?"

"I know why Luinda broke up with you," I said slowly. For a split second, I could've sworn I heard a freight train zooming toward the prison. Everyone else must've thought the same thing, because they were all looking around for the source of the sound. But it was just Hambone on the verge of smashing me through the wall.

"Take it easy, big fella. Just hear me out." I held up my hands trying to calm Hambone down.

"You've been talking to Luinda?" he growled.

"No," I said, smiling innocently. "Of course not." I took another deep breath. "I mean, yes, but she really misses you." I had to talk fast—Hambone's hand had shot through the bars, and he was holding me high above the ground by my shirt collar.

"Start talking, pipsqueak!" Hambone shook me around like a garbage bag filled with marbles.

"She says you don't listen to her!" I screamed. "She wants to talk to you, but you don't seem to understand what she's saying!" My voice was growing higher and higher.

Hambone stopped shaking me and pulled me as close to him as the bars would allow. "She said that to you?"

"Yes." I nodded wildly. "But I think I can help you."

Hambone lowered me to the ground. His body was tense, his face contorted in an angry scowl. "How?" His voice had returned to normal, and he no longer seemed determined to use me as a tambourine.

I steadied my fingers and pulled a small package out of my pocket. Don't ask me why I had Q-tips. I really wasn't sure. I handed the Q-tips to Hambone, and he cradled the white sticks in his hand. He stared down at them for a few moments, and for a second, I thought I saw a smile forming on his hairy lips.

"You think this will get her back for me?" he asked.

Probably not, is what I should've said. "Absolutely," I said instead.

Hambone's eyes watched me closely. I'm sure he was checking to see if I was lying, but I was desperate so I forced the biggest smile I could manage. With the hand not holding the Q-tips, Hambone grabbed hold of one of the bars and yanked it completely out of the wall. Concrete crumbled down from the ceiling and dust rose up from a hole in the wall. Hambone was already bounding away, carefully holding the Q-tips like they were a little lost puppy.

"Good grief, Hashbrown!" Frosty John gasped, standing next to me and gaping at the hole in the prison wall. "You've got some pretty tough friends." He looked honestly impressed.

"I don't think he's my friend. In fact, he's most likely going to smash me into tiny tots when that Q-tip deal doesn't work out with Luinda, but it doesn't matter. I'll worry about that later." I looked at the hole and then back at Frosty. "Shouldn't there be an alarm or something?"

Frosty's tongue stuck out the side of his mouth. "Hmmm," he said. "That's funny. Do you guys hear that pounding noise?" Everyone looked toward the prison cell door. It wasn't pounding, it was running. Someone very big and very scary and no doubt wielding a spatula was running toward our cell.

"Borfish!!" We all screamed. Wasting no time, the seven of us hopped through the hole and charged down the hill toward the playground. It would be empty by now, but that didn't matter. We had to put as much distance as possible between us and Ms. Borfish.

"Where are you going now?" Frankie Folds asked as he ran along beside me.

I wasn't really sure. I hadn't thought that far ahead. "I guess I have to go to Mashimoto's and try to stop him," I said in between breaths. It wasn't a brilliant plan, but it was all I had.

"Mashimoto's the kid with the brand new tree house, right? Over there on LaSalle Drive?" Frosty John asked. He joined me on my left side.

"Yeah, how did you know that?"

"We have our ways." Frosty looked over at Frankie and

then back at the others bringing up the rear. "Are you think-ing what I'm thinking?" he asked.

Frankie nodded.

"What are you thinking?" I gasped, hurtling over a gopher hole.

"I'm thinking you're going to need a little extra help pulling this off. And it seems we have the evening free."

"You're going to help me?"

"Of course, kid. You're the guy that set off the biggest stink bomb in Pordunce history." Frosty smacked me on my back, and I almost doubled over. "What do you say boys? How's about we do a little spy work for our new friend?" The rest of the prisoners cheered.

"Spy work?" I asked, trying to simultaneously control my excitement and not throw up all over the place. "What did you have in mind?"

"Don't worry," Frankie Folds said. "We know just the place."

Chapter 13
Uncle Bilbo's Pitted Prunes

The sun had set, and I shivered as I stared up at the abandoned shack next to Mashimoto's house. This was their bright idea? A haunted house? They were out of their minds.

"I'm not going in there," I whispered, trying my best to keep my voice low and stay out of view of Mashimoto's windows.

"Why not?" Frosty asked.

"Because it's haunted," I said.

Frosty, Frankie, and the other prisoners started to laugh.

Frosty snorted. "It is not!"

"It is too. Look!" I pointed to one of the windows. Even as we were standing there, something was hovering behind the curtains.

"That's just my uncle Bilbo," Frosty said.

"Your uncle?"

"Sure. He's lived here for years. He just doesn't get out much." Frosty John waved to the window, and the curtains fluttered.

"Okay, but what about all the moaning and groaning we hear whenever we walk past this house?" Surely, he wouldn't have an explanation for that. I had been hearing those dreadful noises since I was a baby.

"His uncle Bilbo has irritable bowel syndrome. He has to stay close to a toilet and eat lots of fiber," Salisbury said.

Since I was a little boy, I had believed that house was haunted. Now, not only had I discovered that it wasn't haunted, but it was owned by someone with worse bathroom issues than Whiz. That poor man probably got pretty annoyed every Halloween when my club would light candles along his driveway and shine flashlights through his windows. Oh well, it was a harmless misunderstanding.

We crept across the lawn, and Frosty opened the front door. "Hey, Uncle, I'm home!" he shouted. From somewhere on the second floor, somebody groaned. "He probably won't be coming down anytime soon. I'll check the refrigerator for snacks. You guys go set up by the living room window and see what's going on at Mashimoto's."

Carefully pulling back the curtains, I peered out toward Mashimoto's backyard. From this angle, I could see right up the main staircase of Hi's tree house. It was almost completed. Several cranes rested motionless on the lawn, towering above the beautiful marble walls of the tree house, and a giant satellite dish pointed to the sky from one side. Inside the main entryway, a light flickered as shadows danced around the room. Mashimoto was in there all right, but he wasn't alone. Frosty returned and gave everyone some pretzels before handing me a pair of binoculars. I adjusted the focus and zoomed in on Mashimoto's tree house.

There he was, standing in the center of the room, looking as smug as ever. Suddenly another man appeared. He was tall with long black hair and sunglasses. He was also wearing a laboratory jacket. I froze. Where had I seen him before?

I searched my memory and gasped. It was the Marty

Muffit's employee. I knew it! I just knew he was working with Mashimoto. I covered my mouth with my hand and bit my lip. That dude was spraying blue stuff all over the fruits and veggies!

Just then, the Marty Muffit's employee pulled off his wig and his gleaming bald head lit up the room. I gasped again and swallowed my gum. I hadn't even realized I'd been chewing any. Bubblegum would've been proud.

The Marty Muffit's guy was really the doctor that had made the school visit to Principal Herringtoe. Oh, this was not good. This guy had a million disguises. I was now certain he was also the vending machine guy with the strange new soda pop. In his hand was a beaker filled with a bright blue liquid. What were they doing with it?

I tried to get a better view with the binoculars, but it was difficult. I could tell they were talking to somebody else—somebody sitting in a leather chair in front of them. Then the chair swiveled, and I almost dropped the binoculars.

"No!" I shouted. Snow Cone was tied to the chair. Mashimoto was trying to force Snow to drink the blue stuff. That had to be what was brainwashing everybody. They really were trying to take over the school!

"What's going on?" Frosty asked, nearly choking on pretzels.

"They have Snow Cone," I said, panic rising in my voice.

"Ah, man," Frosty said, still munching. "All we have is some frozen peas. Those lucky punks!"

"Not snow cones," I said. "They have my best friend, Snow Cone Jones, and they're trying to force-feed him some secret potion—the stuff that's turning everyone into raving lunatics!" Salisbury and Tyson the Teapot covered their mouths in shock. "We have to stop them right now!"

"Okay, listen up." Frosty John scanned the faces of his cellmates. "We need to create a distraction so Hashbrown can sneak in there and save his pal. Salisbury, Tyson, and Frankie, you come with me and grab some ammunition. The rest of you, head out the front and come around the far side of Mashimoto's house for an ambush."

"Don't worry, Hashbrown," Frosty said, noticing the frightened look on my face. "This is the kind of stuff we're good at. You're in good hands."

The entire group moved through the kitchen toward the back door.

"You're up," Frankie whispered.

"I'm up?" I had no idea what I was supposed to do.

"Go to the staircase beneath the tree house and hide in those bushes until we give you the signal it's all clear," Frankie said. "Stay low and don't let them see you."

That was easy for him to say. These guys were notorious criminals. They were experts at this sort of stuff. I cleared my mind. *This is nothing*, I thought. *Nothing. It's just another game of paintball, that's all. I'm good at paintball*. I took three quick breaths and shot off toward the tree house. I was like a cat and when I reached the halfway point, my confidence skyrocketed. I did two barrel rolls and then dove over a row of bushes, somersaulting beneath the ladder. No one from inside Mashimoto's tree house had seen me.

Now all I had to do was wait, but for what? I didn't know what the signal would be. Poking my head around the ladder, I looked desperately for Frankie Folds or Frosty John, but they were no longer crouched beside the haunted house. I scanned the yard but found nothing.

Something whizzed through the air and struck the side of Mashimoto's tree house. It was small and black, and it made a rather unpleasant splat when it hit the walls. I craned my neck to see what it was just as several other small objects shot through the air. More and more started flying, and now they had drawn the attention of Hi Mashimoto. I ducked down just as Hi's head poked out the window.

"What's going on out there?" he shouted. About two hundred more small splats peppered the wall. This time I caught a glimpse of Frosty's do-rag as he hid beside a tree. The prisoners were throwing something at the tree house. "Stop it!" Mashimoto shouted even louder.

They threw more. One of the objects dropped next to me, and I scooped it off the ground. It looked like a bug had just exploded, but after closer examination I realized what it was.

A prune.

Uncle Bilbo apparently had an endless supply of pitted prunes, and it looked like they made perfect ammunition. The door above the stairs burst open, and I saw Mashimoto's pink-slippered feet scamper down. He raced out into the yard, still holding his stupid koala.

"Show yourselves!" he demanded.

For a second, everyone did. They stood out from behind the trees and bushes and waved at Mashimoto.

"Who are you people?" Mashimoto asked.

Instead of answering, they pelted Mashimoto with a barrage of prunes. Within seconds, he was completely hosed from head to toe, dripping with purple prune sauce.

"Aaaah!" he screamed, running off into the dark and shielding his head from the continuous onslaught.

The bald mystery man in the white coat was the next to appear from the tree house, but he was ready for the attack. He was now dressed in a white chemical suit and wearing a mask. Hundreds of prunes bounced harmlessly off his armor as he charged toward the trees, hosing the bushes with what looked like a laser gun. Only instead of a laser, his gun shot out a shower of bright blue potion. My new friends didn't stand a chance. They needed help, but I couldn't just blow my cover. Not with Snow Cone still tied up in the tree house.

Just then, the rest of the prisoners circled around from the front. Some were toting large buckets filled with prunes while others flung heaping handfuls of bran fiber cereal. Man, Frosty's uncle really had it bad if he needed that much bran cereal to get things going in the right direction. Armed with their ammunition, my friends closed in on the bald dude. It was the most intense scene my eyes have ever witnessed. There were shouts and screams of anguish as prisoners ran in every direction, trying to avoid the deadly spray. Where was Frosty? Where was Frankie?

It was all-out war, but the bald man was heavily protected under his suit. The bran cereal and the prunes had little effect on him. I clung to the ladder of the tree house, praying that good would prevail, but I knew my friends were no match for this guy.

"Retreat!" Frosty's voice rose above the mayhem, and six do-ragged heads charged through the hedgerow and out of sight. Mashimoto's goon didn't appear ready to quit. Holding his laser up in the air, he charged after them.

The yard fell silent.

As quietly as possible, I scaled the twelve steps of Hi Mashimoto's tree house and slipped inside unnoticed. The tree house really was a masterpiece. Even in these dire of circumstances, I had to have a quick look at Mashimoto's illustrious pad. Sure enough, there was a gigantic plasma television mounted on the wall. Down a hallway, I could see the glow of what had to be Mashimoto's aquarium bed, and resting against the far wall was a large treasure chest.

"Hashbrown? What are you doing here?" Snow Cone asked. He was still tied to the chair, but the blue flask of secret potion appeared to be full. Mashimoto hadn't gotten to him yet!

"Oh, you know, I thought I'd check out the place, play a little pool with Mashimoto. You haven't seen him have you?" I smiled.

"You just missed him. Shucks." Snow Cone laughed.

I knelt by his chair and undid the knots binding him. "Look," Snow started. "I'm sorry about everything that happened the past couple of days."

I shook my head. "It was my fault—not yours. I was so worried about building the time machine that I forgot what was really important." I loosened the ropes around Snow Cone's arms and legs. "But I just knew there was something wrong with Mashimoto."

"So did I," Snow Cone said.

"Well, you could've warned me."

"What do you think I was trying to tell you at the grocery store?" Snow Cone looked at me expectantly.

I frowned. "You didn't say anything. You told me you weren't going to help build the time machine."

"What did I tell you at the very end?"

"Something about buying pickles for my—" I kicked a prune with my foot. How could I have been so stupid? Snow Cone *had* tried to warn me. "Picking up pickles on aisle seven" was one of the original codes in our secret language. It directly translated into "Someone's planning on taking over the world with a secret potion!"

"If I would've listened to you in the first place—"

"We could've stopped all this before things got out of hand," Snow Cone finished.

"But why didn't you just say that? Why didn't you tell me outright?"

"I was being followed by Mashimoto. He thought he was

being sneaky, but that koala of his has a belching problem."

That made sense. It was right after Snow Cone left that Mashimoto had appeared in the grocery store. My pal was brilliant. No doubt about it.

I looked down at the floor. "I really hate time machines."

Snow Cone nodded. "Speaking of which, where did you get that stink bomb?"

"It's a long story." I peeked out the window.

"Well, it was awesome!"

My thoughts flashed back to earlier that afternoon in the auditorium. Oh, the madness of it all! That awful stink! Nothing in the world compared to it.

I grinned. "Yeah, it was."

Snow bent down and picked up a prune. "So, who are your friends out there?"

My friends! They were still being chased by those men. They needed help. "I'll have to tell you later," I said. "Right now, we need to get out of here."

Snow Cone raced toward the far side of the room and jerked open one of the doors of Mashimoto's stainless steel refrigerator.

"Snow, this is no time for munchies."

He pulled out a bottle filled with pink liquid. "We can't leave without this."

"What is it?" I asked.

"It's the antidote. Mashimoto and his scientist were talking about it." Snow Cone handed me the bottle, and I peered through the glass.

"Scientist?" I asked, taking a whiff of the bottle. "I always knew science would be my downfall."

"We need to get that to Ms. Pinkens' lab and see if we can make more of it."

"But I stink at science." I swirled the pink potion around in the bottle.

"Yeah, but Gavin Glasses doesn't."

I smiled. "Right. Okay, you go wake up Gavin, I'll make for the school." I opened the tree house door and started down the stairs. "Whatever you do, don't let Mashimoto catch you."

"Got it." Snow Cone joined me at the bottom of the stairs and started to head for the road.

"Hey, Snow?" I stopped. Snow Cone glanced over his shoulder. "It's good to be friends again." He gave me a fist pump, and we took off in opposite directions.

Chapter 14
A Final Salute

I had walked the halls of Pordunce thousands of times but never this late after hours. The overhead fluorescent lights hummed loudly. It was like I was walking through a mutant alien hornet's nest. I slowly moved through the halls, stopping every few moments to listen for monsters. Knowing my luck, I would trip on something and go flailing down another secret stairwell—one even Luinda Sharpie didn't know about—one patrolled by slime covered turkeys with scales instead of feathers that screeched the word "beware" as soon as you stepped into their territory.

"Stop it, Hashbrown!" I told myself. I wasn't helping my situation by thinking up my worst nightmares.

I arrived at Ms. Pinkens' laboratory and cautiously opened the door. "Hello?" I whimpered, sticking my foot through the opening and wiggling it around. "Gobble, gobble?" I added for good measure. The room was empty.

After resting the bottle of antidote on the counter, I went over and sat in my desk. I felt weird sitting there all alone, staring at the front wall where my drawing of a buffalo still covered a large section of the chalkboard. Where was Snow Cone? Where was Gavin? Shouldn't they be here by now? There was a muffled thud from somewhere down the hallway, and I collapsed out of my desk. It was probably just my imagination. The school was really old. Things probably fell over all the time. I convinced myself to stand and then I slowly opened the classroom door. Sticking my head out through the opening, I looked both ways down each hallway. There was nobody there. I had worked myself up for nothing. One of the air conditioners kicked on down another hallway, and it roared into life. I jumped again but then chuckled. What was there to be scared about? It was just the air conditioner.

No longer afraid, I took a stroll down the hallway. As I rounded the corner heading toward the fifth grade wing, I bit my tongue almost in two.

Standing at the other end of the hallway was my nemesis, Mashimoto. Actually, he wasn't standing; he was hovering three feet above the floor, wearing a shiny, new jet pack. Plus he was still wearing those outrageous pink slippers. Talk about your fashion faux pas.

"There you are!" Mashimoto shouted above the roar of his jet pack. I guess it hadn't been the air conditioner turning on. "Thought you could get away with it, did you?" Smoke billowed out from the rocket boosters on his jet pack. Mashimoto looked like a hummingbird with a bad case of gas.

"Impressive, isn't it?" Mashimoto gloated. "It was made special for me. You could've flown it too, had you simply learned to leave well enough alone. But no, you had to do things the hard way."

I shot a quick glance down the hall behind me—not another soul in sight. My heart thudded in my chest. I was going to have to go one on one with Hi, and that was going to be tough now that he was wearing a jet pack.

"It's time you handed over the antidote, Hashbrown." Mashimoto glared at me. "No more games."

"I don't know what you're talking about," I said as casually as I could.

"Don't play dumb!" he snapped.

"Oh right, that's your game, huh?" I fired back. It was a battle of wits, and I was definitely the wittier one.

I could see Mashimoto's eyes twitching with anger from all the way down the hallway. "Where did you hide it?" He zoomed a few feet closer. I reared back, searching the halls for a weapon. A bat would've been perfect, or a giant-sized fly-swatter.

"What's the matter? Didn't you make more than one bottle? Or did that dork in the white coat spill it all over your slippers?"

"He's a brilliant scientist." Mashimoto glanced down at his pink slippers.

"So, what are you planning on doing after you've brain-washed the entire school?" I asked.

Mashimoto fluttered even closer. "That's none of your business."

"There are better ways to make friends, pal."

Mashimoto's face scrunched up tight. "You think you're so funny, don't you? The great, wonderful Hashbrown! Just because everyone likes you."

"Uh . . . How much of that secret potion have you drunk already? In case you've been absent from school lately, no one likes me anymore."

"Because of me!" Mashimoto seethed.

"Well . . . yeah. Because of you, all of my friends have left my side." Even though, technically, Snow Cone and I were friends again, we had been apart for a good twenty-four hours, more or less, and it was all because of Mashimoto.

"Don't blame me. I just helped your friends truly see the light."

"No, you force-fed them secret blue soda and now they're running around like cross-eyed zombies. I give you no real credit." I glanced down the hallway again. It was just too far. "But honestly, why a secret potion? It seems pretty wimpy if you ask me."

Mashimoto's chest heaved. "For the past two years, I've been trying to start my own club, but you wouldn't allow it. Now, I'm paying you back."

I scratched my head. "What are you talking about? Other than your Grand Gala, when did you ever try to start a club?" I honestly had no idea what he was talking about.

"Don't give me that. I handed out fliers to everyone. We were going to have brownies and cookies, and we were going to play board games all night. But no! Someone had to go and plan club tryouts on the same night, or, better yet, someone had to go and hold an idiotic conference and teach all of our classmates on how to do show and tell seminars. You blew everything. No one came to my parties!"

My mouth dropped slightly open. "Dude, I had no idea," I said, trying to sound as sincere as I could while staring down a fluttering lunatic. "You should've talked with Snow Cone. He's in charge of planning all of our events. We could've rescheduled."

"Don't play nice with me," Mashimoto hissed.

"Seriously, it's not a big deal. I like cookies, and we all know Four Hips does. He's always complaining that we don't have enough catering at our events. There's a better way to handle this."

Mashimoto blinked several times in complete silence. For a moment, I thought he was going to listen to reason. He looked like he was ready to land his jet pack and give up, but suddenly he exploded with anger.

"NO!" His eyes flashed red. "There's only one way to handle this! You had your chance, and now I'm the one who's going to hold the seminars and the tryouts. Not you! And soon, once everyone in the school has taken my potion, I'm going to wipe every memory of you from Pordunce."

"What do you mean?"

"I've already started." Mashimoto's smile twisted wickedly. "Why do you think Yeti was trying to steal your precious little trophy?"

My eyes widened.

"And that was only the beginning. Next time, Teetertotter Williams will destroy your marble hangout. No marbles, no marble tournaments. Whatever will you be famous for?" Mashimoto threw his head back in laughter. "Nothing!"

This was too much. Mashimoto was out to destroy everything I held dear. That marble arena had taken me two years to complete.

Mashimoto was still talking. "I won't need Camo Phillips to change the menu once I have the cafeteria staff under my spell. How do hash browns for lunch every single day sound to you?"

I gasped. "Not that! Anything but that!" I gobbled huge gulps of air.

"So you see, I've thought of everything. Two years, Hashbrown. For two years, I've plotted this very moment when the great Hashbrown Winters would crumble under my power."

I stared at the floor, searching for something I could use to stop him. "Wait a minute," I blurted. "What about the kids that broke into Principal Herringtoe's costume closet? That had nothing to do with me."

Mashimoto bit his lip. "Oh, that? That was nothing. A minor glitch. Something my scientist will work out in time. I'm willing to live with a few students here and there wigging out and playing dress up. It's the bigger picture that matters. Now give me that antidote."

He wasn't messing around. I could tell that at any moment he was going to attack. I decided running was my only option, but I would have to wait for the right moment.

"I got a better idea," I said, inching closer to the far wall and digging my sneakers in, ready to run. "I was being a little rude the other day when I told you that you couldn't come over to my tree house. I should've been nicer."

"Don't try and schmooze me now," he said.

"Just hear me out. Why don't you land that thing and we could go talk about how cool your tree house is."

The jet pack faltered slightly. "You're just saying that because you know I've got you where I want you."

"No, I'm being serious. Look, let's just be friends. I've got another stink . . . er, I mean time machine back at my place. You could come over and . . . um . . . sniff it!" I belted the last words at the top of my lungs.

"Oh!" Mashimoto groaned, balling up his fists in anger. It was my moment, and I took it. I exploded down the hall, running faster than I ever had before, and I didn't look back.

I should've looked back.

If I had, I would've seen Mashimoto charging through the air like a cannonball and I might've been able to duck. Instead, Hi crashed into my back going at least one hundred miles an hour. The jet pack's power immediately shut off, and both of us rolled down the hall, smashing into the lockers. My head was spinning, and tiny, slimy turkeys were swirling around in front of my eyes. Mashimoto would've been dizzy as well, but that goober was wearing a helmet.

Jumping into the air, he landed on my stomach and grabbed my collar. "Ha! I beat you."

I didn't have anything smart to say. I was too dizzy, and Mashimoto must've had rocks in his pockets—he weighed a ton.

"Are we going to do this the easy way? Or am I going to have to force you to obey?" Mashimoto removed a syringe from his pocket—a bright blue syringe.

"Okay, okay, I'll give it to you," I surrendered. What was the use? Mashimoto had the upper hand. He was wearing a jet pack, a helmet, and I'm pretty sure he was also wearing a charm bracelet, but I don't know what that was all about. I stood and balanced myself against the lockers.

"Well?" he asked eagerly.

"It's not here, but I'll take you to it."

He walked beside me, holding the syringe next to my arm like a gun. "You make one false move, and I'll stick you with this," he warned.

We walked down the hall and came to a stop in front of my locker. "Here, I'll get it for you," I said as I started working the combination.

Mashimoto waited, hopping up and down with excitement. "Hurry up," he said.

I tried several times to open the locker, but failed every time. "I can't think straight. My head hurts." I rubbed my forehead. "I always mess up with the combination, but don't worry, I'll get it." I tried the dial again, but it still didn't open.

"Oh, get out of the way!" Mashimoto snapped, pushing me aside.

"But you don't know my combination," I said.

"Yes I do. My scientist stole the master list from Principal

Herringtoe's office yesterday." He waved a sheet of paper filled with numbers in front of my face. "Think I'm stupid, do you? Well, I'll show you." He located my combination on the page. I could see his fingers shaking as he rotated the dial to the left, right, and then back to the left again. The locker gave a satisfying click, and Hi smiled at me sinisterly.

"You see, Hashbrown, no one can stop me. Once, I get this back to my tree house, I'm launching a full-on assault on the school. Things are going to change around here, Hashbrown."

My shoulders sagged. "You're right," I said. "But there's just one problem."

"Really? What's that?" he asked, lifting up on the locker latch and pulling the door open.

"I didn't hide the antidote in my locker."

"Huh?"

He was barely able to finish his word as a tiny tranquilizer dart shot out through the locker opening and stuck into his shoulder. The look on his face was priceless, especially after he collapsed on the floor and started snoring.

"Nighty-night, Hi," I whispered, leaning over to pat him on his helmet. I looked into my locker, and a chill traveled up my spine. Brody the Ape-Slayer with three authentic ninja throwing stars stared out at me from beneath his protective glass holding case. Brody was by far the coolest action figure in the whole state, and I couldn't help but shed a single tear as I saluted.

Chapter 15
Back on Top

"Did you kill him?" Snow Cone asked, staring down at Mashimoto, who was lying on the floor next to my locker. Snow was out of breath from having to run the length of the school. Both Gavin Glasses and Mensa Mike had tagged along.

"No, he'll be fine in about two hours or so." I nudged Mashimoto's limp body with my foot for good measure. "I keep forgetting to reduce the dosage on my tranquilizer darts." I looked expectantly at Gavin. "Can you make more of the antidote?"

Gavin and Mensa swapped a quick glance and started giggling. "Of course we can," they said, amused that I would even ask such a question. They shuffled back down the hallway toward Ms. Pinkens' science lab. Yep, they were dweebs. I was going to have to find a loophole in the rule book to somehow kick them out of my club.

"What about the others? You know, your new friends?" Snow Cone asked.

I gnawed on my lip nervously. "I don't know. Last time I saw them, they were being chased by Mashimoto's mad scientist. I don't know if they made it or not." I was actually worried about them. They had saved my neck. If anything had happened to them, I wasn't sure I'd ever forgive myself. "Are you okay to stand guard over Mashimoto while I go see if I can help them out?"

"Get out of here; I got this," Snow said, grabbing the syringe of blue potion out of Hi's limp fingers. "If he so much as chuckles, I'll stick him good."

When I arrived back at my neighborhood, it appeared every one of my neighbors were out in the street wearing bathrobes and pajamas. The flashing lights of several police cars caught my eye, and those cars were parked right outside my house.

"Trash Clown, how've you been?" Officer Killapup asked as he slapped some handcuffs on the bald scientist wearing the white laboratory coat. "You don't have another time machine on you by chance?"

The scientist wouldn't look up from the ground and kept mumbling something about not saying a word until he could speak with his lawyer. It didn't matter, though. I was sure I could round up enough witnesses once we had the antidote and all of the evidence from Mashimoto's tree house was out in the open. I watched as Officer Killapup forced the scientist into one of the police cars and noticed that the scientist's chemical suit was dripping with a strange yellow liquid. That was funny. The potion was blue and the antidote was pink. Where did the yellow come from? And who had called the cops? It was very convenient, but kind of odd.

"Pssst." I heard a noise from the nearby bushes and ducked away from the crime scene to find Frosty John and Frankie Folds hiding in my mom's mulberry bush.

"Were you able to save your friend?" Frosty asked, his voice barely above a whisper.

"Yeah, I did. Thanks to you guys."

"Eh, don't mention it," Frankie said.

"But how did you get away from that guy? Last time I saw you, he was right on top of you, spraying that blue potion into the bushes." To be honest, it was nothing less than a miracle that Frosty, Frankie, and the others weren't acting like complete zombies at that very moment.

Frosty shrugged his shoulders. "We ran for awhile, and he chased us into a dark alley. We thought we were goners for sure, but that was when Tyson's crow, Grover, swooped in and started pecking his mask so he couldn't see. He ended up uncovering his face when he realized we were all out of prunes to throw. And then the strangest thing happened. Someone stepped out onto the balcony and dumped a barrel of stuff down on top of him. The bald guy started gagging, and it was just the distraction we needed to take him out. But when we looked to see who had saved us, he was already gone."

I thought for a moment. "Wait, you said you guys ran down a dark alley? It wasn't like three blocks that way was it?" I pointed to a neighboring street.

"Matter of fact, it was," Frosty said.

"And were there a lot of dead plants and wilted flowers in the front?"

"Yeah. How did you know that?" Frankie asked.

"That would explain the yellow liquid all over Mashimoto's scientist." Frankie and Frosty didn't seem to follow. "That was Whiz Peterson's place," I said. "He sometimes walks around in his sleep and dumps his bedpan over the side of the balcony."

"Bedpan?" Frosty looked at Frankie and made a face. "But that would mean he poured—"

"Don't," I interrupted, "You don't need to say it."

The siren lights flashed as the police cars started to pull back out of the drive.

"So who called the cops?" I asked.

"That would be my uncle." Frosty pointed across the road to where a police officer stood interviewing Uncle Bilbo, who was wearing a thick wooly bath robe and clutching a giant bottle of antacid tablets in his hands. "He told the police everything, so I think you won't be hearing a peep out of that scientist for a long time."

"That's a relief," I said.

"Is that your tree house over there?" Frosty nodded over to where the rickety wooden steps rose up to my tree house.

I sighed. "Yeah, that's it."

"Not bad, Hashbrown. Not bad at all," Frankie whispered.

"You know, you're right. It's perfect, even without a time machine." I smiled. It really was the best hangout in the whole neighborhood. "Hey, do you guys want to be members of my club?"

They all looked at each other, and I could tell they didn't seem up to the idea.

"Nah, we got to get back and start fixing up that hole your buddy made in our wall," Frosty said.

"What do you mean 'get back'? You mean to the prison?" No way were they heading back to Pordatraz. They could go free and enjoy the good life.

"We're not ready to be out just yet," Frosty said.

"Yeah, all the flashing lights and the big buildings—it's kind of scary," Frankie said. "It's a lot different from when we were first locked up."

"The world's got real big in a hurry, Hashbrown, and we're not ready to catch up with it." Frankie stood and watched as the last police car drove out of view.

"So you'll just go back to prison?" I asked, still not

understanding why they would ever think that was the best thing to do.

"Yep. But you can come visit us from time to time," Frosty said. "And maybe we can join your club when we get paroled in a year or two."

"If you say so." The three of us shook hands.

★ ★ ★

A few days later, I was in my normal spot at our lunch table. Snow Cone sat next to me, sipping his chocolate milk. Beside him, all the rest of my club filled up the other seats. We were back together again. Every one of them, with the exception of Snow Cone, had drunk the secret potion. After they took the antidote, it was my turn to apologize. I returned our eggs to their secret stash beneath the tree house and vowed never to turn my back on my friends again. We decided to forget everything that happened in my tree house on that fateful night when I went berserk, and then we mostly shared stories about where everyone was sitting and what everyone was doing when the deadly stink bomb struck. It was legendary.

You're probably wondering how I got out of my prison sentence. Well, I owe Frosty John for that. After the prisoners patched up the hole in the wall, Frosty asked for a free phone call and called his Uncle Bilbo. It just so happened that when Bilbo wasn't downing prunes and fiber cereal, he was a very successful lawyer. He negotiated my sentence down to a harmless one week's worth of detention learning about law enforcement with Officer Killapup.

As I chewed on a piece of roast beef, Hambone appeared in the cafeteria holding hands with Luinda "The Manatee" Sharpie. That was a beautiful sight. Partly because I wouldn't have to run for my life from Hambone for at least another month or two, but mostly because those two were made for each other. Hambone got my attention and winked. Was it possible he and I would become friends? Don't get your hopes up. Lightning doesn't strike twice unless your name is Weather Vane Dane. I had to squint, but I noticed a new piece of jewelry dangling from both their necks. Most couples wore those cheesy heart necklaces. Theirs were a little different. Two white Q-tips swished back and forth on their chains.

Hi Mashimoto was allowed to come back to school under close supervision. All of his new toys had been taken by the authorities. The construction crew was still at work in his backyard, but instead of completing the dream tree house, they were taking it apart.

In a way, I feel sorry for him. It really was going to be the coolest tree house in the whole school, but that doesn't matter to me anymore. I have my health, and I have my friends. . . .

Ha! Sorry. I can't pull that off.

I'm actually throwing a good-bye gala in my backyard later this week to celebrate the destruction of Mashimoto's tree house. Come on. Don't judge me. He's the one with the criminal record, after all.

All right, relax. I know it's kind of my fault that all this happened in the first place. If I had been more sensitive, I would've noticed Mashimoto and made an effort to go to his parties. I guess I'm not perfect. Sure, he tried to take over the school and brainwashed all of my friends, but I can't completely blame him. They *are* cool friends. And I know it was because of Hi that I landed in Pordatraz Prison, but if I hadn't, I would've never met Frosty John and Frankie Folds. To be honest, I'm really glad things ended up the way they did. That's why this weekend's party is going to be great. There'll be pony rides, a cotton candy machine, and maybe even a waterslide. Whiz is all geared up and ready to go. It's going to be expensive, but I'm sure the club can all agree on letting me bust open at least one of the eggs for such a worthy cause.

And this is the best part: I'm going to make Hi Mashimoto my guest of honor. I know what you're thinking: *Wow, what a noble gesture.* It's the least I can do. I'm even sending out special invitations to everyone in the school. I've already sent one to Mashimoto. It's waiting outside his front door, and I even wrapped it in a special package. He's going to be so excited. I mean, who wouldn't be thrilled to look down on your porch to see a beautiful, shining, silver ball with bright colored buttons? I can hardly wait to see the look on his face.

Wisdom of the Oracle: A Top-Secret Guide to the Riff Raff at Pordunce

Well, well, well, back for another round of ridiculous adventures, are we? Honestly, the students at this school are getting weirder and weirder by the minute. If you're ever passing through the area and decide to stop to take a tour (don't know why you'd ever be so foolish), be sure not to drink the water. Somebody dumped a whole can of moron juice in the reservoir years ago. Of course, you can see for yourself.

Yeti Mckean (Adam Douglas), 5th grade: Since when did burlap pants become popular? Oh, wait a minute, Yeti always wears shorts. Ms. Borfish once punished him for not eating all of his lunch by throwing him into a sink filled with greasy dishes. The pots and pans have never shined so bright.

Moses Merryweather (Steven Cobble), 4th grade: Wannabe. Imposter. Don't get me started on that loon! Just give me five minutes alone with him in front of my locker. I'll poke that fake beard right off his face!

Gavin Glasses (Cole Robertson), 1st grade: Yes, he's smarter than most wizards, but really what has that brain of his accomplished? Daily phone calls from NASA and an honorary membership in Hashbrown's club? Please! I hardly call those achievements.

Hi Mashimoto, 5th grade: Oh, I'll admit I was excited about Mashimoto's Grand Gala, but you try squeezing your way through two miles of air conditioning duct. It's not pretty. Well, at least I have this delicious piece of blue pizza to nibble on. I've always liked that Mashimoto. . . .

Humus Laredo (Orville Granola), 5th grade: As far as I can tell, he's not human. Anyone who eats birdfeed and soy milk for lunch is from another planet. Oh, and I'm pretty sure tree-huggers don't really hug trees.

Tyson the Teapot (Elroy Hutchings), 4th grade: Short, stout, and incredibly ornery whenever he's near a sauna. He's an absolutely horrible checker player too.

Gurgles Dunderland (Albert Joe Dunderland), 4th grade: Don't be deceived by his nickname. Gurgling is not what I would call the noise coming from that boy. If your washing machine made half the sounds his stomach makes, you'd throw it in a ditch.

Echo Rodriguez (Ronald Rodriguez), 3rd grade: He once got in an argument with himself which started a feud for over a month. He had to use Pigeon Criggle to send messages back and forth to himself until finally he—they? oh whatever—worked it out.

Brandy Newspickle, 5th grade: One of the local pretties. Always smiling, giggling, and batting her eyelashes. I grow nauseated with it all.

Squeaky Mittons (Dennis Tibbs), 3rd grade: I swear we've tried everything to rid that boy of his squeaking. We don't even know where the sound is coming from.

Weather Vane Dane (Ian Dane), 2nd grade: All I have to say is Weather Vane is forbidden in the third grade wing.

That lightning rod of a kid is bad news for anyone trapped inside a metal box.

Yankee Molicka (Chester Molicka), 2nd grade: His excess earwax means he never has to worry about putting in ear plugs whenever Ms. Borfish brings out her megaphone. Matter of fact, none of the students in the second grade have to worry about putting in earplugs when Yankee's feeling generous.

Tuna Fish Marrero (Albacore Roderie), 5th grade: It's one thing to bring a dead tuna for show and tell, but it's a completely different thing to wear the dead fish on one's hand like a puppet during the school's Christmas concert, pretending that it's the Ghost of Christmas Past.

Fibber Mckenzie (Alex London), 5th grade: In his defense, Fibber's not really sure what the truth is anymore. Rumor has it, he was abducted by aliens at a very young age and had his brain altered so that he had no choice but to lie about everything. Of course, I happen to believe that Fibber started that rumor.

Frosty John née **Salami Johnson** (Hank Horace Johnson), 6th grade: By now you've heard how Frosty got his name, but few people remember him when he went by Salami Johnson. Back in those days, I was locker-free and it was perfectly normal to throw cold cuts at the lunch lady when you ran out of chocolate milk.

Cup o' Noodle Hickok (Richard Elroy), 5th grade: He was always complaining about having to walk to school in the winter, so he came up with the brilliant idea of filling his pants pockets with hot soup to stay warm. Boy, did he love the idea. Now, even in the summer, you can smell a strong odor of noodle soup wafting from his jeans.

Salisbury Dickory (Colby Trey), 6th grade: Of all the stupid costume choices for Pordunce's Halloween Party, his takes the cake, or should I say steak? He even forced some first grader to walk around with him dressed as a large can of gravy.

Mensa Michaels (Benjamin Victor), 1st grade: Supposedly he's pretty good at math, halfway decent in chemistry, and can recite all of Shakespeare's plays from memory. But can he stuff a microwaveable pizza through a locker slot? Nope. Moron!

Wombat Willie (Wayne Workman), 6th grade: No one believed him when he said he had a real live kangaroo stuffed under his jacket last year at football tryouts. That was until Vice Principal Humidor got booted through the goal posts when he made the mistake of getting too close and barking like a coyote.

Wish-Bone Parker (Chad Wayne), 4th grade: You'd be able to do the splits too if you were dumb enough to try and return a mechanical pencil to Luinda "The Manatee" Sharpie's school store. Now, Wish-Bone can kick a whistle out from between his own teeth.

Frankie Folds (Lewis Nuttermeyer), 6th grade: Not a very good poker player.

Discussion Questions

1. Hashbrown starts quite a mess when he lies to Hi Mashimoto about having a time machine. Have you ever told a lie that got you into trouble? What did you have to do to fix the problem?

2. What happens when Hashbrown becomes more interested in building the time machine than listening to his friends? What would you do if you had made your friends so mad they didn't want to hang out with you anymore?

3. Why do you think Snow Cone never gave up on Hashbrown, even when Hashbrown said some really mean things? Do you have a friend like Snow Cone?

4. One of the coolest things about Hashbrown's club is his secret code language. If you had a secret code language that only you and your friends knew, what would be the five most important phrases you would use and what would they mean?

5. Pordunce Elementary is not your typical school. What makes Pordunce so different? What would you think if your school had secret stairwells? Or a playground prison?

6. In *Hashbrown Winters and the Mashimoto Madness* there are a lot of strange, new characters introduced. Who was your favorite? And who would you like to read more about?

About the Author

Frank L. Cole was born in a quiet town in Kentucky where he spent most of his childhood sharing exaggerated stories for show and tell. He now lives in Utah with his wife and three children.

One of Frank's greatest claims to fame was when he was rushed to the emergency room as a third-grader after falling out of Hashbrown Winter's tree house. If he had a nickname it would be Frankie the Phantom.

Check out Frank's first novel: *The Adventures of Hashbrown Winters* and be sure to visit him online at:
franklewiscole@blogspot.com
and www.hashbrownwinters.com.

0 26575 53788 8